SASH

FAY

EROGENOUS ZONES
BOOK THREE

FAYE'S SPIRIT
Erogenous Zones Book Three

© Saskia Walker

First published in 2012
This edition © 2014 Saskia Walker

This is a work of fiction. Names, characters, places and incidents are solely the product of the author's imagination and/or are used fictitiously, though reference may be made to actual historical events or existing locations. Any resemblance to actual persons, living or dead, business establishments, events or locales is entirely coincidental.

This book is not transferable. It is for your own personal use. If it is sold, shared, or given away, it is an infringement of the copyright of this work.

Please note: this book is for sale to adults only. It contains sexually explicit scenes and graphic language which may be considered offensive by some readers.

Cover design by Frauke Spanuth at Croco Designs.

FAYE'S SPIRIT

Chapter One

Faye Evans rapped the heavy wrought iron knocker three times then quickly consulted her notebook as she waited for the door to be opened. The client's name was Garth Connors, an architect. Apparently Mr Connors had sensed paranormal activity in his recently refurbished office space, a rather impressive building in Highbury, North London. Faye was there to find out whether anything could be done about it. Mr Connors had seen her advertisement the week before and asked her to come over at the close of business on Friday.

Tucking her notebook into her shoulder bag Faye pulled her coat collar up to ward off the late winter weather and studied the building. It looked Victorian, with smooth grey stone slabs on the facade of the ground floor and plain stone above. It was tall, at least four floors high, from what she could see in the streetlights. Slim pillars flanked the doorway and the windows were uniform, elegant sash affairs. It wasn't what she'd expected. She'd wrongly assumed an architect would have his office in a modern building. Perhaps a healthy respect for historic buildings came with the job description. Did it indicate that Mr Connors was a stuffy sort with half-moon spectacles and a bow tie? He didn't sound like that on the phone. He'd been charming and had even flirted with her a little.

She was about to knock again when the door opened. A tall, rangy man stood in the doorway talking into his phone. He held up one hand in her direction, as if to request a moment to complete his call. Faye used that moment to give him a thorough inspection. He was dusky skinned, with shaggy black hair and brown eyes that were almost black. A narrow soul patch ran from his sensuous lower lip to his chin, emphasising his lean jaw and giving him a gypsy-like appearance. An open necked, crisp white shirt revealed a nicely muscled chest, and the shirt was worn loose over snug fitting jeans. His black leather cowboy boots made her smile—quirky and attractive, not stuffy at all.

The project suddenly seemed even more interesting.

"Hold that thought," the man said into his phone when he finally looked her way and engaged with her. "I'm going to have to call you back." He switched off his phone and shoved it into the pocket of his jeans. With one hand outstretched, he smiled broadly. "You must be the expert on spooks."

Faye took his hand. "And you must be Garth Connors."

He held onto her hand and drew her closer, gently urging her toward him in the most provocative way. Instead of answering her question he gazed down into her eyes. His smile was gorgeous, a well-practiced charm that nevertheless melted her to the core. Faye warmed right through. She was about to make a joke about him keeping her on the doorstep when another man appeared at his side.

The other guy looked at her then frowned at the man next to him. "Jai? I thought you were on your way home."

The gypsy-looking man shook his head. "I'll stay a while longer. Think I need to know as much about this ghost stuff as you do." He still had hold of Faye's hand and he squeezed it. Humour flitted through his expression.

Faye couldn't help chuckling.

That drew the attention of the other man.

"You must be Faye." His expression lifted when he looked at her and he put his hand out, forcing her to break free from the first man to shake his hand. The new arrival was tall and built like a rugby player, with broad shoulders and a powerful grip. His closely cropped hair was a warm brown, almost chestnut coloured.

"You're Garth?"

His green eyes crinkled at the corners. That was one lovely smile.

"Yes. I see you've already met Jai." He pronounced Jai like *Chai*. "Jai is my partner."

Faye's attention sharpened. *Partner?* She couldn't help being intrigued. Both her sisters were involved with men who'd been partners before they met her siblings. The suggestion that these two were lovers instantly triggered Faye's libido. It also launched her imagination into an entirely more intimate scenario.

While Garth turned and ushered her inside, giving Jai a nudge on the shoulder to get him to move, she pictured them stripping off, the gypsy looking man—Jai—perhaps using his shirt to playfully whip the big guy across his rather fit arse. She attempted to quash the inappropriate image, but it was too late. Her imagination had become fully engaged, and as she stepped inside the house her gaze roved over them both, picturing them naked and aroused.

Jai made a big play of staring at her as if rooted to the spot, undisguised interest in his eyes. Garth was more subtle but he took a good look at her too. While Faye walked into the hallway, making her way between the two tall male bodies and beyond, she had to suppress her smile.

The two of them had a brief mumbled conversation behind her, which gave her a chance to look around the interior of the building. It was warm and inviting after the cold outside and the smell of fresh paint lingered in the air. The floorboards in the hallway had been stripped back but were as yet unvarnished. It was an impressive town house with high ceilings, an ostentatious hallway and a double width staircase. At one time this had been a wealthy Victorian family home. Was that when their resident spirit had locked on to the place?

"Let me take your coat." Garth appeared at her side.

Once she'd taken off her coat he gestured to the front room, which turned out to be a reception area with a desk and several comfy armchairs, all of which appeared to be brand new and unused.

What caught her attention most of all was at her left side, because the entire back wall of the room had been replaced by a glass panel, through which she could see their workspace. Computer screens and drawing boards and scale models of buildings were on display to the occupants of the waiting room. "Oh, wow. That's quite a startling sight in a house like this."

"That's just the reaction we want people to have coming in here," Garth said, while he put her coat on a stand behind the door, "the promise of an exciting and unexpected development." He beamed at her as if she was an exciting and unexpected development too.

"Great idea. It really does have a huge impact as you walk in." So impressive that it almost diverted her attention from the double dose of powerful male testosterone that surrounded her—but not quite. Faye was too busy bathing herself in that to be distracted from it for long, and Garth gave it out in droves. He was a mere foot away, but swayed closer as he looked down into her eyes.

"I'm so glad you approve," he murmured.

"Oh, I do."

"You're just as I pictured you would be, when I heard your voice."

"What, a kooky psychic chick?"

"No, not at all." He grinned, but didn't comment further. The way he looked at her assured her he liked what he saw.

Jai followed them into the reception area, his boots clicking out a dramatic staccato soundtrack on the stripped floorboards as he walked. The guy was barely tamed looking, and the boots echoed his personality. He folded his arms loosely across his chest and observed the two of them.

Garth looked at him with a mildly querying expression, as if surprised he was still there. Jai really had been on his way out of here, she realised. Well, she was glad he stayed. The presence of two such interesting men was a rare treat. Mostly because she'd been working two jobs for the past eleven months, which didn't leave much time to meet people. Three days a week she worked in an esoteric knick knack shop to help cover her bills. The rest of her time, including evenings and weekends, she'd been trying to kick-start her ghost connection business. Lately that had taken off, because one satisfied customer put the word out and her business started to look good. However, it also meant she didn't have much time to meet men, while both of her older sisters had no shortage of them.

"Everything really is all shiny and new." She nodded at the chairs, where scatter cushions were still wrapped in protective cellophane.

"Yes indeed, but we're just about ready to go now." Garth was clearly dying to show the place off, ghost or no ghost.

"Did you have another office before this one?"

"Not one of our own," he replied. "We've worked together in a larger company since we graduated." He picked up a cardboard box that sat on the reception desk and showed it to her proudly. Inside the box lay a brass plaque, a door plate. "This is about us starting out on our own as a new partnership."

Faye stared at the object, reading over it.

"This will be going up outside the front door next week and then we're ready to cut the tape and welcome clients in."

Garth Connors and Jai Nilsen. Chartered Architects.

Below each of their names was a list of letters that she assumed were their qualifications. They worked together. As it sank in, she realised she'd made an inaccurate assumption about them.

"Oh." Her face heated rapidly. "You're business partners." As soon as the words were out, she wished she hadn't spoken. The comment made her look like a right twit. Her embarrassment deepened and she pressed her lips tightly together, not trusting herself to speak. She looked from one to the other of them. They weren't partners at all, not in the sense she had imagined. She'd only gone and barked up the wrong tree completely because of her sister's relationships.

"Yes." Garth's eyebrows drew together as if he confused about her meaning.

"You thought Garth meant we were *partners*," Jai said, and he elongated the word for emphasis.

Faye felt as if her face was on fire. "Well, this isn't awkward at all is it?" She laughed at herself. "Sorry. Oops."

The penny dropped with Garth. "Good God, no, not like that."

"Just good friends," Jai added, but his eyelids had lowered and he watched her with interest.

"And new business partners," she hurriedly clarified. "Got it."

Garth returned the brass plaque to the reception desk then shoved his hands into the pockets of his trousers. "Don't let us to keep you," he said to Jai, and adopted an overtly masculine pose, widening his stance, with his shoulders pushed up and back.

Faye fought back a nervous giggle.

"You're not keeping me," Jai reassured him. "I'm intrigued." He looked back at Faye. His dark eyes gleamed and her embarrassment quickly faded as she realised he wasn't bothered. If anything, he was amused and entertained by her assumption.

She felt little bit less like she wanted the floor to open and swallow her up. Besides, even if they weren't lovers they were both gorgeous men in their own way. Her lewd imagining of Jai whipping Garth's arse as he chased him around a bed was off the mark, but fun nonetheless. And she wanted them both to stay. Perhaps that had something to do with the fact they were both looking at her as if they wanted to leap on her to prove they were straight and fully operational in the pleasure-a-woman department.

She restrained a smile. *I'm imagining it, just because Monica and Holly have had a threesome, doesn't mean I'm ever going to get the chance.* "Have you both sensed the presence of the ghost?"

Garth nodded.

"In that case," she responded, trying not to appear too eager, "it would be ideal if you were both here while I make some notes."

The men exchanged glances. Jai made it known that he was pleased by the turn of events. Garth didn't look as sure, but shrugged it off.

"Perhaps we could get comfy." She drew Garth's attention back. "Is there somewhere where I can make notes while we talk about your resident ghost?"

Garth brightened. "The staff room. It was the old kitchen in the original house and we've kept that function. We put in a table and chairs for informal meetings."

"Sounds perfect." She followed Garth, noticing again how broad his shoulders were. Jai brought up the rear. When she inhaled deeply, she found herself intrigued by the combined aromas of their chosen colognes—sandalwood and musk for Garth, and something exhilarating, reminiscent of the seashore, from Jai.

"Actually, this is where we've both sensed the ghost's presence most of all," Garth said as they entered the large kitchen area. "Here and on the staircases."

Faye nodded and studied the place. It had been updated in line with the rest of property, but with more basic furniture, giving it a more practical look than the public areas of the building. A large table in the centre of space was the focal point. "Yes, I can sense some residual paranormal activity in here."

She crossed to the sink. A big picture window there overlooked a backyard. It was hard to see how large it was, in this light. A sturdy door in the corner opened onto the same. Once she'd got her bearings, she stepped behind the table and put her bag on it, lifting out her notebook, pen and phone as she did so.

The two men took seats opposite her. Faye liked the arrangement, because it meant she could look at them as they chatted but she could also see into the hallway beyond. If anything non-corporeal stirred, she'd sense it. She opened her notepad and brought up the Internet on her phone. "So, I suppose we better get down to business."

Both men looked at her expectantly. Jai sprawled back in his chair, one arm latched over the back rest as he got comfortable. Garth rested his elbows on the table and stared across at her. For a moment she stared back, enjoying the attention. The interest definitely seemed to be reciprocal, if she wasn't misjudging things. It could be simple curiosity about her work, but she was aware of them looking at her even when she looked down at her notepad and dated the page. It made her remember sidling between the two of them as she'd entered the house. All that masculinity, surrounding her. She squeezed her thighs together under the table. That only made the wild tingle of arousal between them worse.

Focus, she told herself. She was here to work. "Can I begin by asking what you know about the history of the house?"

"It was built in the 1850's," Garth replied.

"1850's right. Do you know anything about the people who lived here before you bought it?"

Garth shook his head. "The place stood in complete disrepair when it went to auction. Apparently it'd been a family home for most of its history, but it had been abandoned and let go derelict for the last forty years."

"Interesting." Faye drew herself a quick time-diagram of occupancy with the approximate date noted alongside it. "What a waste of a great building while it was empty."

"That's what I thought," Garth said.

"The place was a nightmare when Garth got the keys," Jai interjected. "Woodworm and dry rot and damp."

It sounded as if he hadn't approved of the purchase to begin with. Faye scribbled on. "Do you know the reason why it was left derelict?"

Garth shook his head. "There weren't any details in the estate agent's information package."

There wouldn't be, if some sort of a drama or tragedy had happened in the house. Faye didn't verbalise her thoughts on that score, but she picked up her phone, opened her favourite search engine and tapped in the street address. She continued to chat as she looked over the links that appeared. "It can happen that way, if people can't live with the paranormal activity. Is your ghost noisy, I mean does it throw things around?"

"What, you mean like a poltergeist?" Jai trailed his fingers back and forth over the raw wood of the table while he spoke.

It was an overtly erotic gesture, making her wish those fingers were trailing on her naked body instead. She found it hard to concentrate, because both of them looked as if they'd much rather be flirting than talking facts about the building. An undercurrent of sexual interest traversed the table, ricocheting between them. Occasionally the men would glance at each other, Garth with an almost territorial look in his eyes.

"Yes. That can sometimes put people off buying a house if it had that kind of heritage." She twisted her pen in her hand, weaving it between her fingers.

Jai watched.

Something about the simple habit she had of playing with her pen made him look brooding, his sensuous mouth pursed.

"Any physical description for me?"

Jai met and held her gaze.

Garth pulled himself together to respond. "I've seen something moving in the periphery of my vision, and Jai has a sense of when she's in a room, but she's never clear."

"But you're sure it's a woman?"

Jai nodded. "Somehow it *feels* that way, and there's the cheap scent, very blousy and floral." The way he said 'feels' was deliberately suggestive.

Faye wrote it down. "She has a distinctive perfume, how intriguing. That must have been an important part of her corporeal persona if she has carried that with her."

"This is too weird, talking about it like this." Garth ran his fingers over his short cropped hair, making Faye want to do the same.

"Don't worry, I'm used to it." She gave him a reassuring glance.

"It's not even as if we've really seen anything specific, is it," Jai said.

Garth agreed. "With me it's just like I get the feeling someone is there and see something from the corners of my eyes, but when I look properly I see nothing, even though I feel as if I'm not alone."

"It's similar for me," Jai continued, "but with the scent."

Faye noticed how easy they were with each other, how their comments rolled from one to the other. "Does it make you feel uncomfortable, or afraid?"

"No. It's more that it's weird," Garth said, "you know, kind of eerie."

He probably wouldn't have admitted fear anyway, but she felt he was being up front on that score. He seemed like a straight-forward kind of man. What it indicated to her was that the spirit wasn't giving off malevolent vibes to them as the new occupants. "Is there a particular time of day that she appears?"

Garth replied without hesitation. "Late at night, always. We were working elsewhere and checked on this place at night while the renovation was being done, and that's when we started to notice."

"Anyone else caught sight of her—that you know of?"

They were silent a moment then Jai spoke up. "One of the builders made a joke about it. He told us he thought the place was haunted when they came back to pick up their gear."

"Yes," Garth agreed, "that's what got us thinking we ought to investigate before we open the office formerly. What with our own odd feelings about a presence and his comments, it began to become an issue."

Faye nodded. "When will you officially begin working from here?"

"Monday after next, nine days away," Garth replied, "although I've started living in the private accommodation on the top floor."

"Ah, so you're already resident." That meant at least one of them wouldn't be rushing off to a home elsewhere. If she had to wait around for the spirit to make an appearance some company would be ideal, especially two such intriguing men. Just then she felt her skin prickle and her perception shifted. There was indeed a paranormal presence in the building.

"We've got a receptionist lined up to start next week," Jai stated, "but I made a joke about the place being haunted and she freaked out. I had to pretend I was kidding to stop her running off on us. That really motivated us to get this sorted before opening."

"I can see that would be a problem. You don't want your receptionist shooting out whenever she hears a creaking floorboard." She chuckled. "It pays to have good sense of humour in this job."

Both men nodded. Faye had grown used to people treating her warily, as if she were a bit of a nutcase, a hippie freak, but these two seemed to like that about her.

"You seem confident about your work, are you always successful?" Garth moved the conversation onto more personal ground, and he seemed genuinely curious.

"Mostly, yes. There was this one case I was involved in where a ghost lingered on after I'd been there. It was a difficult one, because the ghost had attached itself to someone who was still living. Its presence did diminish though, and I still visit there to see how things are. I'm hoping that we can work toward a quick result to enable you to open up here without concerns." She paused and thought about the next statement. "I can already sense the paranormal activity in the house, in case you were wondering. It's increased since I arrived."

"Impressive," Jai commented. "I'm not getting anything outside of what's shooting between the three of us."

Faye almost dropped her pen.

He grinned.

When Garth looked at him questioningly, Jai shrugged it off.

Faye couldn't help laughing. His comment thrilled her to bits. "Back to our ghost, do you get any sense that she's unhappy that you are here, that she might resent you being in her house?"

Garth looked surprised. "*Her* house?"

"As she was resident here first she may think of it as her home and that you have invaded her space. Has she been negative toward either you in any way? Slamming doors, cold draughts?"

Both men thought about that for a while then shook their heads.

"That's a good start. She likes you." She paused to smile their way, braving herself to match up to them.

They both smiled back.

"We'll need to find out why she lingers, in order to usher her on her way. It helps if we don't start in a war zone." She moved on quickly in order to take the edge off her comment. The last ghost she had interrogated had been hugely put out about being requested to move on. The case had taken much longer than the weekend she had scheduled, and she hoped the same wouldn't happen here. Although being around her hosts would make up for that, if it did happen.

They stared across at her while she made her notes. She gave herself a moment to absorb the feeling of having two men focused on her in unison. No wonder her sisters liked it so much. Would she ever get a little taste of that kind of intimacy as well? One glance in Jai's direction made her think he would be up for it. Jai flirted openly, engaging with her every time she looked up. Garth was more of an intense kind of man, but he was forthright and that had its own appeal. The fact that they were straight also fascinated her. Nevertheless, they were more than business partners. The quality of their relationship reinforced the fact that they'd known each other for a long time. Had they shared women before, was that what she sensed?

Just then something on her phone caught her eye and she opened up the link. She scanned the information quickly. "Did you know that your property used to be a brothel?"

"No, seriously?" Jai spoke, but when she looked at Garth he was more than a little startled too.

"It's amazing what you can find out on the Internet these days. You can check it out yourself, now that you know." She continued to scan the information. "It looks as if the place was boarded up and left to rot when the brothel was shut down in 1965. Other than that, no tragedies show up on an initial scan."

When she saw the querying glancing in Garth's eyes she attempted to explain further. "The reason spirits linger is often because they have an unresolved aspect of their life that they can't let go of."

She didn't want to bring the mood down, so she put her notepad away and switched her phone off. "Now all we have to do is wait for the ghost to make contact with me. As I said on the phone, you don't have to wait with me."

She said it as a courtesy, in case they had real partners to return to, but she was delighted when they both turned down the opportunity to leave.

Garth leant forward. "No, I'm happy to stay with you."

"It's a real pleasure," Jai agreed.

"No loved ones waiting at home?"

They both shook their heads. For a moment they exchanged looks across the table, before the conversation moved on.

"Are you sure you'll be able to make contact with the ghost?" Garth asked.

"Oh yes. I will see your ghost." She enjoyed the curiosity in their eyes. "Don't ask me why, but it's been that way ever since I was a kid. If there's a spook around I can see them and I can communicate with them. It took several years for my family to realise that I didn't in fact have imaginary friends but ESP, and it was actually the spirits of those who had gone before that I was chatting with."

"That's some special talent," Jai said.

"Like I said to Garth when he called me, it's weird, but if I can help people—and spirits—with this gift, why not."

She could tell that Jai wasn't a sceptic. He had an esoteric aspect to his personality, especially in comparison with his colleague, Garth. Jai was free spirited. Garth was a bit more down to earth. They were like two sides of a coin, friends who functioned well together because they brought different attitudes to a situation.

When she smiled at the thought, Jai cocked his head on one side and narrowed his eyes, as if he was trying to guess her thoughts. Then he rose to his feet. "If we're camping out here for the evening, I'll go get us some takeaway food and some wine."

Garth stared up at him. "Aren't you going home?"

"Are you kidding, with such good company"—he nodded at Faye—"and the possibility of finding out about the resident ghost?" He turned his attention back to her. "Is Chinese good for you, Faye?"

"Sounds great, thank you."

He gave a slight bow. "My pleasure."

Mine too, she thought to herself, her anticipation growing by the moment.

Chapter Two

Jai deposited the bag of take-out food cartons on the worktop next to the wine carrier, lifted out a bottle and went about looking for the bottle opener. A glass of wine or two was just what this situation needed. "Where's our guest?"

"*My* guest." Garth checked out the cartons then took several plates and some cutlery over to the table. "I gave her a tour of the building and now she's freshening up."

Just as well, Jai thought to himself. Garth needed a talking to. He prowled around and growled like a territorial big cat. "What's your problem?"

Garth gave him a deliberately disbelieving look. "You stayed behind because you're interested in Faye."

"Yes. So?" He took in Garth's frown. "Oh, I see, you're assuming that just because you hired her you've got first rights at chatting her up?"

Garth had a strict code of honour and any suggestion of working a system to gain an advantage made him uncomfortable. Jai knew that and he liked to tease him about it. "Come on," he said, and put his free hand on Garth's shoulder, "she's flirting with both of us. Chill out and enjoy it. It's just a bit of fun."

"What, you really want me to compete with you?" Garth shook his head and gave a gruff laugh as if he secretly liked the idea of the challenge.

Jai studied him a moment before answering. "If you have to see it that way, fair enough. As I said, I think it's a bit of fun. Something we can share, perhaps."

Garth stared at him as he processed the comment.

Jai could see his message was beginning to take hold.

Garth shrugged, which dislodged Jai's hand from his shoulder. "You're a kinky freak," he said in a low tone, and glanced at the door as if he watching out for Faye's return.

"That's one way of putting it," Jai responded, "I suppose. You should try something a bit kinky, you might like it."

"What makes you think I haven't 'tried it'?"

Jai arched his eyebrows. "I think you'd have mentioned it, besides, I haven't heard that strict upbringing of yours snap and unravel and I've been listening out for it, believe me." Jai gave him a sideways grin to lighten the comment.

"So you have to come from a modern extended family to have an open mind about sex, is that what you are saying?" Garth looked positively enraged by the suggestion, which amused Jai all the more.

"Extended family? Why not say what you mean? You'd call it a broken home. My parents divorced. I'm chilled about it and so are they. I have stepparents as well as real parents. We're a diverse, multicultural group but we're happy."

Garth looked a bit sheepish at that point, as well he might. "Sorry, I didn't mean that to sound quite the way it did."

"Look, buddy, I have no idea why I'm more of a free thinker than you," Jai continued, "but I do know that it's not too late for you to loosen up and live a little."

"I live plenty. Life isn't just a list of sexual experiences you have to tick off. What if you meet someone you really respect? You have to start off on the right foot."

"And what if kinky sex *is* the right foot, when you meet the right person?" Jai knew he was being provocative, but he couldn't resist. Garth's eyes flickered, as they often did when his mind raced. "Sometimes you've just got to go with the flow and see what happens," he added.

Garth threw him an accusing glance.

Jai felt startled by the sudden intensity of what he saw there, and it struck him that there was more to this than he'd first thought. "Wait a minute you're not still angry about Izzy, are you? I thought you'd dropped that old grievance years ago."

"I have dropped it. It's just that this situation reminded me of it. I meet a woman I like, one who seems interested in me, and suddenly you're there, Mister Charm personified stealing her from under my nose."

"Izzy was the only one, as far as I recall." Was this really the right time to talk about the Izzy incident, Jai wondered? It had been years back, and she hadn't been mentioned for a long time. Perhaps he shouldn't have mentioned it now, but Garth was obviously still thinking about it.

They'd been students when Garth had dated Izzy, but she'd gravitated to Jai and Garth had been left cut up about it. They'd settled back into their friendship when Izzy had moved on. She'd headed to Paris for her European study abroad and never returned. Since then they had a strong—if competitive—friendship.

However, it looked as if he should address this old grievance or it would spoil the evening, and he didn't want that to happen. Besides, Faye had flirted with them both. He tried to keep his response light. "Anyway, I'll have you know I actually met this lady before you, I got to the door first."

Garth shook his head. "Unbelievable."

"Lighten up."

Garth rolled his eyes. "We chatted on the phone, I liked her then."

"Get real. You can't fall for someone over the phone."

"We had a rapport. I knew we'd get on."

It started to make sense for Jai. "That's why you were ushering me on my way this evening. It was because Faye was coming over. I did wonder."

"Do you blame me? Any chance for you to get your leg over and you're in like Flynn."

"I enjoy women. That's not a crime."

Challenge flashed in Garth's eyes and his mouth lifted at the corners. "Maybe you should let her decide."

Jai was fascinated by this edgier side to his old friend. They enjoyed sparring and this was a whole new game. "Maybe we should."

Garth opened a drawer, lifted out a bottle opener and extracted the bottle of wine from Jai's hand. "And, trust me, if she is interested, I'm not giving up on this one without a fight."

Interesting. Garth really had grown a backbone since Izzy. Jai couldn't help smiling. Garth had walked away from the Izzy situation once he knew she was interested in Jai too. Garth hadn't taken kindly to the suggestion that all three of them got it on together—a suggestion that had actually come from Izzy. Izzy had wanted them both. Garth was too traditional to give it a go though. Had he ever had the chance of three in a bed again? Jai didn't think so. Would he have the backbone to give that a try now? Jai's curiosity built.

"I love it when you get all competitive on me." Jai winked at his buddy. The urge to compete hadn't harmed them in business, quite the opposite in fact. "That's why we're so good together. Nothing like two front runners to set things alight, huh."

Garth pulled the cork from the wine and reached for a second bottle. Determination shone in his eyes and a mysterious smile hovered around his mouth.

Jai lowered his voice another notch when he heard Faye's footsteps descending the stairs. "Game on?"

Garth nodded. "Game on."

Jai's anticipation sharpened.

"Oh my," Faye said as she walked into the kitchen, "that does smell good."

Garth turned her way and smiled. "Hungry?"

Jai noticed that Faye's voice had an immediate effect on Garth's expression. The big guy really did like her.

Faye sidled over, looking from one of them to the other in an overtly flirtatious way, and nodded. "This all looks wonderful, thank you."

She was definitely interested in them both. Was she keeping her options open until she got to know them better, or was she looking for something a bit more kinky, like Izzy had been all those years ago? Jai gave Garth a sidelong glance. Garth returned it with a weighty stare. The gauntlet had been thrown down. For a moment Jai felt as if he should walk away —let Garth pursue the lady all by himself, make up for the Izzy days—but his competitive spirit wouldn't allow it, and when he looked at Faye he didn't want to leave. She intrigued him. Besides, it would be interesting to see Garth fighting his corner.

Often, when they took on a joint project, they egged each other on like this, with good results. This was a bit more personal, but…all the same, it made Jai wondered how things would turn out.

Faye quickly took charge of the food, opening up the cartons and lining them up on the table. Garth sprang into action and got some glasses out. Jai poured the wine. The kitchen became a hive of activity, but when Faye glanced at either one of them—and she did that often—the atmosphere became more heavily laden with sexual tension.

Jai couldn't have been more pleased.

Once again Faye sat opposite them, and this meant he could watch where her attention was focused. Everywhere—from Garth to him then down the hallway, where she was presumably watching out for the ghost. While they ate she quizzed them about their work and their hopes for their new business, but all the while she seemed to be on high alert for the invisible occupant of the house.

"I didn't realise dinner and wine was included in this commission." She had a naughty look in her eye when she brought the conversation back to the current event.

The Lady was playful. Jai liked that.

"If we have to wait for the ghost to flit through again," Garth said, "we might as well get comfortable and enjoy the company."

Garth really had invested himself. Jai accepted he had some serious competition here.

"I appreciate that." She dabbed the corner of her pretty mouth with her napkin. "There's definitely a paranormal presence in the house." She gestured with her napkin then ran a finger around the top of her wine glass. "But it's best to let it make itself known to me when it feels like it."

"And they always show themselves to you, it's intriguing." Jai was fascinated with her talent. Anything unique drew him like a glittery thing called to a magpie. He was all about edgy and new experiences.

She sipped her wine then nodded as she put the glass down. "Oh, there was this one occasion. The ghost didn't reveal itself to me for two days. I think that the client, a mature lady, had begun to think I was only there for her wonderful post-world war Britain childhood stories and her lemon drizzle cake." She paused. "It was good cake though, and eventually her resident spirit made an appearance."

Jai was willing to bet the lady she spoke of had enjoyed Faye's company. He certainly enjoyed it and Garth obviously did too. The good food and the wine had mellowed the mood, but the sensual indulgences heightened the sexual tension, just as Jai knew they would.

Faye had harnessed his curiosity as soon as he saw her on the doorstep. Although she had a Bohemian sense of style she seemed very grounded and practical, which was a curious mix. Most of all, her responsive nature beckoned to him. The woman had an obvious sensual appreciation of everything around her, and he was dying to know what was going on in her thoughts. She kept looking at both of them as if running some inner commentary, and he would have paid highly to know what she was thinking.

Her lower lip was full, and it made Jai want to kiss and suck her mouth, to enjoy the wine on her lips. He wondered what she would look like naked. His gaze drifted over her torso and he hardened, because he could picture her sitting astride him. He had the feeling she would look elegantly elfin even while shagging.

She seemed to sense his thoughts had wandered into the arena of sexuality, because she stirred her fork above her plate and looked his way with heavy lidded eyes. Did her psychic powers run to reading minds, or was she just attuned to the erotic suggestion between them? It wasn't something he'd considered. This was one sexy lady.

It was time to edge things forward.

"I'm curious. You thought we were partners in a relationship. Did you really think we were gay?"

"Yes, I'm curious about that as well," Garth said, "do we really look like a gay couple to you?"

Faye's mouth twitched at one corner. "Actually, I didn't think you were gay. More like bisexual." She lifted her glass and sipped from it again, eyeing them over the edge as she did so.

Jai knew an aroused woman when he saw one, and she was enjoying this. "Go on."

She shrugged, and her eyelids lowered as she focused on her glass in the table. Still the smile hovered around her mouth.

"Tell us why you thought that," Jai encouraged. "More to the point, why don't you tell us why that interested you so much?"

Her eyelids flashed up and she stared across at him, her lips parted as she addressed the undertone in his questioning.

She was about to spill. He was sure he was on the right path and he had this hunch about what was going on in her mind.

"You're a forthright woman," he added. "You told Garth here he hadn't done his research on this place." Jai nodded his head in Garth's direction.

She chuckled softly, and he noticed her breathing pattern had altered, because her chest rose and fell rapidly. The rise of her breasts beneath her silky dress caught his attention. In her cleavage, the skin shone in the light from the overhead spots.

"Oh, it's just because I know someone who is involved with two men." She looked across at them for their response.

Jai's interest was already piqued, and now it was growing.

"What, you mean they have someone on the side?" Garth asked.

Sometimes his old friend could be slow on the pickup. Jai blamed that on Garth's strict upbringing. It left him bewilderingly innocent of the kinky goings on in the world. He fiddled with his wine glass, wanting to edge it on, but knowing Garth needed to grow into this comfortably if it was going to move forward at all. "My guess is Faye means her friend has two men at the same time, am I correct?"

Her pupils had dilated. She nodded.

"Tell us more, I'm fascinated." The fact she was interested in it and had deliberately mentioned it turned him on. He enjoyed women who were open about their needs and desires when it came to bedroom matters. Of course Garth might not be able to handle it this time either, if she actually said it aloud, but that was a risk he was going to have to take to find out more juicy details.

She took a deep breath, but then faltered and seemed to freeze before she spoke. She glanced left, past them, into the darkness of the hallway beyond the kitchen.

That's when Jai felt it, exactly what he'd felt on several occasions before. The atmosphere changed, tightened somehow, as if an external force shot tension through the air. He felt a presence at his back and the smell of that cheap perfume. Their resident ghost was somewhere in the vicinity.

Faye looked back at them. "Keep talking to me," she said beneath her breath. "Don't stop."

Chapter Three

Right when the conversation ended up getting interesting, Faye sensed the spirit who occupied the house emerging from its history and materialising in the present moment. The two men seemed unaware at first, but the telltale signs that she always got hit her before anyone else realised the spirit was there. The atmosphere became alive with psychic information that ran along her nerve endings and drew her attention away from the delicious scenario opening up with her two hosts. She felt unwilling to lose the impetus of the moment and she was torn, but when a ghost present she was unable to do anything but engage with it.

"Keep talking to me," she whispered as suggestively as she could, and winked at them.

"I figure I'm right," Jai said, who latched on to her message. "Two men at once, that's what Faye means. Three in a bed."

"Okay, I get it," Garth replied.

Three in a bed, with these two. Faye's pulse tripped at the idea of it. What with that and the psychic activity in the room, she felt positively wired—lit up like a Christmas tree.

Peering into the gloomy corridor she saw the ghost materialising. Jai was right, it was a woman. At first Faye saw her as a haze of light, then as a figure outlined in a halo of luminosity in the darkness. As she moved closer to the area where they were gathered, Faye again urged the men to keep speaking while she concentrated on the paranormal occupant of the house.

The first thing she noticed was the woman's style of dress. Because it was a Victorian house Faye had expected someone from a more distant historic era. Instead the woman wore fashion straight out of the 1960s. A fuchsia coloured mini dress that was edged at the hemline and neckline with black.

Her hair was piled high on her head with a corkscrew teased down on either side, framing her face. The most striking thing about her, however, was the way she was focused on the two men.

"It depends on the line up." Garth's voice reached Faye.

Jai managed to catch her eye. "That probably goes without saying. We'll have to ask Faye more about her friend."

"I'd love to chat about it later." She smiled.

While the two men had a rather staged conversation about threesomes, Faye watched. The men's presence here attracted the spirit by the looks of it, and she moved toward them with anticipation, craning her neck as if to get a better look. There was a fondness in her eyes, and as she passed Garth, she moved her fingers around his shoulders, not quite touching him, but the desire to do so was there. Then she moved closer to Jai and studied him from one side.

For Faye it was blatantly obvious how interested the ghost was in the two men. Despite everything that happened at once, Faye found that amusing. She could hardly blame the woman, after all. Perhaps the presence of the two attractive men also accounted for why it took the ghost a few moments to notice the third person in the room. When she did, she glanced quickly at Faye, pursed her lips as if annoyed, and returned her attention to Jai. Then she paused and looked again, and her eyes rounded. She gripped her hand against her chest as if in fright.

Oh yes, now you see it, don't you. Faye nodded her head in the direction of the ghost, holding the ethereal spirit's gaze.

The ghost, however, was so startled that her lips moved in a silent curse and she completely evaporated from view a moment later.

"Damn." Faye sat back in her chair. The ghost had quickly developed a case of annoyance or shyness when she realised she was being watched. It was often the way. The spirits she encountered were initially startled that she could see them and communicate with them.

Faye felt an echo of the frustration and shock the ghost had felt. Such was her psychic link with the spirits she encountered. Meanwhile, the men were attempting to carry on their stilted conversation about threesomes, which hooked her just as badly.

"Two women?" Jai shook his head. "It doesn't have to be. It depends on the chemistry and the set up, more than anything."

"I agree." Faye interjected. "She's gone now." She rose to her feet. "You were right, it's a woman, from the sixties if I'm not mistaken, and she's fascinated by what's going on here."

"Aren't we all," Jai commented in a low, suggestive tone.

Faye arched an eyebrow. "I meant she's fascinated by the new residents, not the talk of threesomes."

"Shame," he murmured, watching her from under heavy lids.

Boy, was that a sexy glance. "You're so bad," she shot back.

What with the adrenaline rush she got from interacting with the ghost, and the three-way arousal simmering in the atmosphere, she felt electrified by the adventure. She stepped across the kitchen, heading for the corridor where the ghost had disappeared.

As she passed, Jai reached out and grasped her hand, drawing her to a halt. "It's not just the ghost you're interested in, is it?"

Faye's arousal flared. She felt light-headed from the rush of energy all around her, both paranormal and physical. Thrown by his directness, she struggled for a response. "Well, I am here to sort out your ghost problem." Both men watched her avidly. *You can do better than that*, she told herself. *Be brave.* "Although I'm just as intrigued by other things here too."

With that she pulled her hand free and headed into the darkness of the corridor, following the path the ghost had taken.

Two chairs scraped against the kitchen floor behind her and both men were quickly on her heels.

Faye's self-awareness level ticked higher still. This had turned out to be more interesting than any other commission she'd had. She took a deep, steadying breath then reached up and ran her hands along the wooden banisters on the staircase in the hallway, trying to sense if the spirit lingered, and if so, where.

"What are you doing?" Garth asked.

"Just checking to see if she's hiding out here, observing. It's sometimes quite a surprise for a spirit when they realise that I can see them." Did the ghost have a bolthole, a favourite place to hide? "Did you say you felt her mostly on the ground floor?" She glanced over her shoulder only to find both men inches from her back.

"Yes," Garth replied, and Jai nodded.

That might be the case but the ghost was gone, well and truly vanished into the ether—for the time being at least, shocked by her own visibility to a live person. Meanwhile, two much more immediate entities demanded her attention.

Faye turned toward the two men and rested her back against the wooden banisters. Both of them were close at hand, and they were looking at her the way they had been when the discussion about threesomes had been launched minutes before. As her eyes grew accustomed to the gloom in the hallway she noticed how intense they both looked, exchanging the occasional glance as if silently conferring. Was it her imagination or was that what they were doing? Was their bond of friendship strong enough? She wished she had her sister

Holly's knack for gauging people's motives. Holly was much more gifted in that department than she or Monica.

Jai leaned closer to her. "Do you think she'll come back, now that she knows you can see her?"

"I'd say we give it a few hours. Once she gets used to the idea she'll either find it appealing or she'll get angry, depending on her character."

Jai gave her a slow, seductive smile and looked at her in a way that made her body heat with arousal, almost as if he had touched her.

"A few hours, huh." He stepped closer, wrapped his hand around the wooden strut at her side, then stroked her hair through his fingers with his free hand, following the line of her bob down to where it curved beneath her chin. Garth, meanwhile, had a brooding look about him that said more than words. The man wanted to touch her the way his partner had.

Faye grew dizzy with the sheer erotic potential. Both men had their attention locked on her, as if they'd barely been distracted from the sexy banter by her wispy encounter with a being from the past, and appeared to be waiting to resume their intimate conversation about threesomes. Had they done this before, she wondered. Had she fallen into the ideal situation to live out that fantasy that had rolled through her mind and body for the last year?

Jai seemed to be all for it. Garth held back a tad more, and she sensed he was still disgruntled that Jai hadn't left earlier. Nevertheless, the brooding passion in his eyes assured her he might be interested in playing along, Jai or no Jai.

"Hey Garth," Jai said, as if grabbing the moment and moving things along, "perhaps we can take the rest of the wine up to your apartment and chill out there for a while."

On her earlier tour she'd seen the place was open plan, with a bed so handy it was blatantly suggestive. "I can pop back down later if I sense her lurking about."

Jai moved his fingers from her hair to her neck, and stroked her there, making an intimate connection. He spoke without taking his attention away from her. "I think it sounds like a great idea, don't you, Garth?"

Tension emanated from the spot where Garth stood.

For a moment she thought he would say no, then he reached for her hand.

Her heart tripped a beat.

Clasping her hand tightly in his, he nodded. "Allow me to lead the way."

Garth couldn't quite believe it. He'd scarcely welcomed his companions into his private apartment space at the top of the building and Jai had managed to get Faye into his arms. Garth had been ready to play along, to let her know he was every bit as interested as Jai, even if he hadn't been so obvious and hands-on about it. Now it felt as if he'd had the rug pulled from under his feet, because Jai had got the advantage.

He'd known that Jai might push it forward and quickly, and Garth already felt out of his depth, but the turn of events left him speechless. Garth had been pointing out the way to the top floor bathroom then turned around to see it unfold before his very eyes. Faye stepped in, looking around the place admiringly, the colour in her cheeks high and her eyes bright. Jai was close behind her and when she stumbled on her heels, Jai was right there—scooping her into his arms from behind and steadying her on her feet.

Fair enough, it was the right thing to do.

But Jai didn't let go. Instead, he clasped her tighter to him and danced with her body spooned against his. When she let out a gasp of surprise followed by a mischievous giggle, Garth was mesmerised by the way she looked in another man's arms. The way they moulded together, like two familiar lovers, made him want to hold her that way too. Somehow Mr Charm had slipped in and beaten him to it. He couldn't believe this was happening again. It was like reliving the Izzy disaster all over again.

Faye wasn't Izzy though. Izzy had been a wild child, into everything. Faye was a woman. *I want her, badly.*

From the moment he'd heard her voice he'd been intrigued. She managed to sound fun and reassuring at the same time, and when she arrived the attraction quickly solidified. He hadn't felt like this in a long while. The hint of mischief in her expression attracted him most of all. She was all woman too, her pretty frame softly curved beneath that floaty dress she had on—the dress that Jai currently stroked over her hip with one hand.

Say something, you fool, Garth urged himself. He could cope with that, he had to stay on the ball. "Are you okay, did you trip on something?"

"I'm fine. I just caught my heel on the door plate." She seemed keen to reassure him, but there was a distinct breathiness to her tone, as if she was aroused by Jai's hands on her.

"I'm sorry about that. I'll have to check it out. It might need to be adjusted."

"Music, we need music," Jai murmured, but he didn't make a move to do anything about it, just threw the suggestion out there.

The sense of injustice Garth felt kept him rooted to spot, unable to do anything but watch as Jai turned Faye around in his arms, making her face him—still dancing their hips together all the while—and when he got her exactly where he wanted her, he ducked his head down and touched his cheek to hers, dancing on.

Faye responded. She wrapped her hands around Jai's neck. He nuzzled beneath her jaw, apparently kissing her there.

Garth cursed silently, wishing that he'd at least had a chance to put some more lights on. The spotlights from the kitchen area were on and that sent a mellow light into the seating area. He liked it that way on an evening, whilst winding down, but he felt the urge to switch more lights on and shock Jai out of his role as primo player in the house. They were barely inside the door. If he didn't take action soon he'd be forced to leave them alone. That was the last thing he wanted to do.

Before he had a chance to make that move and flood the place with light, Faye turned and locked eyes with him, and it changed everything. The look she gave him made him reconsider. Half-lit, she looked so damn sultry. The lights were perfect as they were. There was an invitation there in her eyes. She didn't want him to leave them alone.

Garth couldn't walk away.

Jai lifted his head too and without breaking the entwined embrace they were locked in, they both stared Garth's way.

Expectation built in the atmosphere.

"Our host looks as if he thinks he's missing out on the action," Jai commented.

Garth gritted his teeth, determined not to let Jai rile him, not now. Instead he studied Faye, wanting to know her thoughts, determined to do so.

She nodded at Jai's comment, but she didn't break the eye contact she maintained with Garth.

Garth clung to that. "You're my guest. Are you comfortable with this…situation?"

After a long moment she responded. "I think so, if you are?"

Her voice trembled slightly, but she wasn't under pressure. Was Jai right, did she want them both? Was she kinky that way and, if so, what did she want exactly—a threesome, or someone to watch her getting it on with Jai? The questions flooded his mind, and Izzy strolled through his confused thoughts again as well, making him question his own motives.

This was not about Izzy. That much he knew, despite Jai's suggestion that it was. He was a different man now and he wanted Faye.

Still Jai stroked her body, shifting the fabric of her dress as he did so, making the hemline shift higher. Garth couldn't have turned away even if he wanted to, because he wanted to touch her the way Jai was, maybe lifting that dress high enough so that he could cup her bottom and lift her against him. It struck him how easily he could hold and carry her—and wrap her legs around him—if she wanted him to. His cock hardened.

When Jai kissed her neck again, her head dropped back. Her breasts buoyed against the fabric of her dress—and against Jai's body.

The tension in Garth's shoulders built. His spine grew ramrod straight. He wanted to cause that reaction in her, he wanted to feel her body ripple under his hands as he kissed and stroked her and made love to her.

Jai moved, turning Faye to face Garth more openly. Jai stood behind her with his hand wrapped around her waist while he kissed the side of her face in a playful, light-hearted way.

Fuck him. Garth couldn't be like that with a woman, not right away, and Faye was enjoying what Jai was doing to her. What chance did he have?

"Perhaps Garth is enjoying seeing you this way," Jai said, loud enough for everyone's benefit, "and who could blame him, you're a very attractive woman."

Garth battled with his self-control. Why couldn't he be more like Jai? He wanted to go over there and grab her into his arms, but he was afraid that if he did he might be tempted to thump his old friend in the process. "You're being deliberately provocative, Jai."

Faye shifted within Jai's grasp. "I thought you two had done this before."

Nonplussed, Garth gave her a querying look.

"Shared a woman," she added.

Jai only seemed to thrive on her remark. He locked both arms around her waist and watched Garth over her shoulder, his mouth curved at one corner. "You like the idea do you, the idea of Garth and I sharing a woman?"

"Yes, but I thought that's what you…" Her voice trailed off and her eyelids lowered. Her cheekbones coloured.

Garth could see that Jai stroked her again, moving his hand over her hip bones. He rocked against her from behind. Garth curled his hands into fists. She would be able to feel everything against her back, and Jai was bound to have an erection. Christ knows he had one, and he wasn't even touching her.

"No, we haven't shared a woman." Garth put it out there, needing to state that truth, but perversely also wanting to push things forward. What with his urge to compete with Jai and sexual desire feeding his thoughts and actions, logic and reason were slipping from his grasp. "Why, do you want that?"

Her eyelids lifted. "It was a fantasy of mine and when I met you, I thought…" The colour on her cheeks heightened. "I got the impression that maybe you had."

"Just because we haven't, doesn't mean we never would." Jai moved his fingers to her chin, turning her face to his and kissing her on the mouth.

Garth's cock ached within the confines of his clothing—his balls tightening, his body readying for sex—even while he wondered if he could live up to her fantasy. Sharing a woman with Jai? He'd thought about it, because of Izzy, but he never really believed it could happen. And still he doubted his own motivations. *Too long without a woman.* But no, he still wanted her. Her tinkling laughter, her grounded words and that flashing smile magnetised him.

When Jai drew back he looked Garth directly in the eye. Slowly that dress of hers had shifted up her thighs. "I'm sure Garth would like to see what you look like when someone is making love to you."

Garth caught sight of over-the-knee stocking tops and purple lace panties, and he lost it. "I would like to see that," he said, overly loudly, "but I'd rather be the person who was making love to her."

It came out of nowhere, but Garth couldn't help himself. He had to have his say or this thing would be out of his control.

Faye moaned softly.

Despite the frustration he felt he could see that Jai was pleased by his response. Garth twitched with annoyance. He was being drawn in but he resented the feeling that he was being manipulated by his more experienced friend. "Show some respect. Faye is our guest, not a plaything."

Jai gave a husky laugh. "Well, Faye, your honourable host is worried that you aren't happy about this. If he could feel the energy coming off you," he paused and ran his fingers from her chin down her neck and into her cleavage, before cupping his hand around one breast, "I don't think he'd have any doubts."

Garth ground his teeth, narrowing his eyes as he observed.

Faye's eyelids lowered and she moaned aloud when Jai's hand moved around her breast, holding her through her dress. "I'm okay," she murmured, panting for breath, and looked at Garth. "Don't worry." Then she reached out her hand to him, her fingers beckoning to him. "Please, come closer."

Pure, primal lust surged through Garth.

"You are such a temptation." He whispered the words under his breath, never thinking for a moment she would hear him.

"This situation, that's the temptation." Her expression showed him how much she wanted them both.

Garth crossed the space and somehow he was up against her. He'd closed the gap. His aim was to draw her away from Jai, but Jai seemed to be so much better prepared. He still held her by the shoulders, kissing her collarbone from behind, pushing aside the fabric of her dress to enable him to access the soft skin there. Garth kissed her, locking his hands around her waist.

Her lips parted under his.

He was swamped in her, and it was everything he wanted.

She shifted and wrapped her hands around Garth's shoulders while leaning back into Jai, and Garth felt what Jai had referred to—her willingness to be with them both. Jumbled thoughts made their way into his consciousness. It should be wrong. It should feel wrong. It wasn't meant to be this way. One on one. *This was too kinky. Shouldn't have drunk so much. How strong was that bloody wine anyway?*

Nevertheless his cock felt rock hard inside his trousers and somehow the way Jai held her against him made it feel so much more intense. He ran his hands down from her waist and around her hips, daring to lift her from the floor for a moment before resting her back on her heels. What he really wanted to do was wrap her legs round his hips and carry her to the bed.

Jai seemed to offer her to him. It jarred. But he wanted to master his insecurity, had to. Faye was willing. Despite his reserve, the need to experience this had him firmly in its grip. She wanted it. He'd be a fool to deny it now. She was moulded around him, her womanly body keyed to his, one knee lifted against his thigh, ready for the taking.

Like she would be with Jai if he still held her?

The thought of Jai making love to her as well made him falter. Jai would do it, if that's what she wanted. Garth braced himself. He had to taste her first, before Jai. Perversely, the thought of Jai getting intimate with her as well made his cock harder still. *What the hell? Losing it now.*

Faye locked her hands around his hips, and his cock pressed against her abdomen. Her tongue stroked over his, inviting him in, the warm damp heat of her mouth making him think of easing his cock into her pussy as well. Meanwhile, the soft feminine curve of her belly seemed to give, to cradle his erection, which showed him how much he wanted to be inside her—really inside her. Cursing silently, he wondered what the hell had got into him. No woman had made him lose it that his way, not ever. The need to be buried to the hilt inside her made him reel out of control, yet his fundamental moral character demanded he was proper and true.

Breaking the kiss, he jerked his head back. "I'm sorry, but you are turning me on big-time."

She looked up at him, and her eyes were almost solemn in their intensity. Her cheeks were flushed. Mascara streaked beneath her eyes, making her look foxier still. "Don't be sorry," she replied, lifting her chin as she did so. "I'm not."

One glance at Jai assured him he was on the right path. Jai nodded at him, somewhat frantically. On some level it irritated Garth that Jai could be so sure, but he needed it—he needed Jai's re-assurance that this could work.

Accepting it without further question or self-examination, he touched her ear lobe, shifting the pendant earring there back and forth in order to help him focus. "Sweetheart, if you don't want this to happen, you're going to have to say so now, because I want to be inside you and I'm in danger of losing what little self-control I have left."

Mischief flitted over her expression. "What if your ghost appears?"

He had to make a supreme effort to clear his head for a moment to figure out what she meant. Then he felt ashamed of himself for having forgotten the real reason she was here. The look she gave him was so playful that he quickly pushed that shame aside. He knew what he wanted. He was sure now. "The ghost can wait."

She shook her head. "Ghosts who materialise can never wait, let that be known…but ours has run away for the time being, now that she knows I can see her."

She issued the warning then she snuggled closer.

That action made him breathe deeper, steadier—surer. The ball was in his court, he had to return the serve. "In that case we better move quickly, because I don't want to be interrupted by a ghost while making love to my ghost hunter."

"Yeah, the ghost is going to have to get in line," Jai commented from behind.

Garth threw him a warning glance before he looked at Faye.

She caught her bottom lip between her teeth. He could see she wanted it all, and that she was amused too, and he couldn't help but be infected by it.

"This is crazy," he muttered, with a disbelieving laugh.

She nodded. "Yes, crazy, but good."

Chapter Four

Faye was adrift on a tide of arousal, and Jai just kept nudging her further out to sea. Garth offered to steady her, but he was also the hesitant one. She wasn't naturally adept at sensing people's thoughts and moods the way her sister Holly was, but it was written all over him that he had to be sure. The man was charming in an old-fashioned way, and it made her reach for him. Tipping her head to look up at him she shook her hair back. "Take me to your bed, please."

"Faye…"

She stood on her tiptoes. "I want you," she whispered, close against his ear. That did it.

Garth meshed his fingers with hers and led her toward the far end of the apartment, where a floor to ceiling wall of glass blocks cordoned off the bedroom area. He flicked a switch on as they entered the bedroom, and twin lamps lit either side of the bed. The simple, wine coloured bedding and blonde wood frame made her pause. Was she really going to get naked on that wine bed with him, and Jai?

Garth seemed to sense her hesitation and paused.

She didn't want to stop. *Couldn't. Not now.*

Pulling him closer to the bed, she found herself backing him against it. They were ricocheting together, both of them battling doubts and yet driven by desire.

He sat down on the bed then reached under her skirt as he looked at her. She stepped between his open legs. The feeling of his touch on her thighs made her pulse race. He looked at her with steady determination, stroking his hands up the back of her legs until they rested in the crease beneath her bottom.

From somewhere beyond music started up, and she realised there had to be a speaker in this room. Jai must have put a CD on. She didn't recognise the music, but it was sexy and seductive and stirred her in all the right places.

She swayed, then lifted her dress in her fingertips and pulled it up, over her head and off. As she dropped the garment to the floor, she heard Jai enter the room behind her. Was that the heat of his stare she could feel, or her own sense of self-awareness going into overdrive? Whatever, it made her burn up from the inside.

"You're beautiful." Garth covered her erect nipple with his mouth through the lacy fabric of her bra, even while he reached around to get the bra undone.

The heat of his body and his actions infected her, and she moved her hands over his shoulders, relishing the strength she felt there and the way his muscles shifted as he worked to unhook the bra. When he pulled the straps from her shoulders, she instinctively held the loosed fabric against her. It felt significant. Once the bra had gone, she'd really feel naked and exposed.

When she let it drop, Garth cupped her bared breasts.

Faye melted under his touch, savouring it while she looked over at the man who leaned up against a chest of drawers in the gloomy corner of the room, observing. Two such different men, both seemingly available to her. Was it a dream? She ran her hands over Garth's shoulders and up the back of his neck, watching as he licked her nipples, assuring herself it wasn't a dream. It was real. Deep at her centre her pulse ticked furiously, wiring her whole body with sheer physical need.

Garth's fingertips paddled along the band on her panties, teasing her skin, making her long to be completely naked when he clutched her body close to him. The hard virile strength so close at hand made her dizzy. He looked up at her while he moved one hand between them and ran his knuckles over the bump of her pussy through her undies. The contact was tentative, exploratory, but it made her body sing.

"Please," she whispered breathlessly.

"Oh God, yes." He stretched the fabric to enable him to put his hand inside and curve his hand over her pussy.

Faye gripped his shoulders tightly and rocked her hips to him, needing more. Trapped between his legs and barely able to keep still, her body was in an acute state of arousal. Garth slipped one finger into her damp niche, and when he made contact with her clit she moved restlessly, shifting her weight from one foot to the other. She pressed her fingers into his shoulders, craving him, her body eager to be wrapped around his, to feel that masculine flesh against hers—his body working into her, his cock filling her.

Then she looked beyond him at Jai. What was he thinking? "Are you just going to stay there and watch?"

He responded without hesitation. "No."

The deliberately provocative statement—with all its promise, its eroticism and its mystery—stole her breath away.

Jai's expression filled with wicked intent. He was going to watch them, but he was going to join in too.

Forcing herself to inhale she wondered how she would cope, then she knew. *Just let go, just let it happen. Just do it.* She liked that last one most of all. *Just do it.* Hadn't it been her fantasy, one that they were helping her to make real?

"Do you have a condom?" She had to vocalise the question, because pretty soon they were going to need it. "As in right now?"

Garth reached over to the bedside table and scrabbled through the drawer for several seconds before emerging with a box of condoms. When it opened, they flew everywhere. Faye grabbed one, and handed it to him. "Put it on, quickly."

When he took it from her fingers she reached for the buttons on his shirt, plucking them open. He assisted, shrugging the shirt off. Her hand went to his belt, and when she felt the hard shape of his erection pressing against the zipper she couldn't get to it quickly enough. For the past few minutes—since they'd come upstairs—it seemed as if everything went in slow motion. Not anymore.

She kicked off her high heels and rolled off her stockings while she eyed his body eagerly. His shoulders and chest were strong, dusted with dark hair. Garth had torn his shoes and socks off and as he dropped his trousers, the sight of his snug black shorts and muscular thighs made her want to clamber all over him.

Pulling down her panties, she cast them aside.

When she looked at Jai, he raised his eyebrows appreciatively.

I'm naked in a room with two men, two gorgeous men.

Her heart hammered in her chest.

Garth had pushed down his shorts, stepped out of them, then rolled a condom onto his erection.

Faye stared. It was gloriously erect, and so big. *Just do it.*

Once he'd rolled the condom on and anchored it at the base of his cock, she put her hand on his chest and pushed him so that he dropped down and onto his back on the bed, then she clambered over him.

Straddling his hips, she cast her hair back and closed her eyes for a moment, bracing herself. Then she felt the hot weight of his sheathed cock against her pussy and she didn't think about it anymore, she just acted.

Crouching over him she kissed his mouth then took his cock in her hand and guided it to her sex. The broad head stretched her open and she lifted away from his kiss, groaning with pleasure as she eased down onto it.

It felt so damned good, hard and hot and rigid as iron. He moved his hands to hold her, to steady her as she moved fully into position.

"Oh, that's good."

"You bet it is." His head went back, his neck arching as the head of his cock met her deep inside.

He filled her completely, stretching her. "Fuck, I feel dizzy."

She could barely pant for breath. Her nipples were diamond hard, the skin on her torso fast growing hot and damp as her body responded to the glory of being filled. She swayed on him, and he acted, holding her hips tightly to him—maintaining the intimate sexual contact—he rolled her onto her back and took charge.

Winded by the sudden change of position, Faye all but fainted into the bed. Garth rearranged her legs round his hips and began to drive and thrust with barely repressed vigour.

"Sorry," he blurted, "the way you feel, I just had to move."

He'd been holding back, but he wasn't holding back anymore. Piston like, he thrust into her. Like a man possessed, working fast and hard.

Faye's breath caught each and every time he pulled out, before driving back in and filling her to the hilt.

"Tell me if it's too much," he added.

"I think I can just about cope." She widened her eyes at him and smiled, and he took it as encouragement, because he worked her even harder.

Faye moaned and writhed on the bed. She couldn't see Jai, but knew he watched—watched her being fucked by his best friend. She flung her arms back on the bed, glancing down to look at the point where they merged. Her breasts were outrageously peaked, her legs splayed, her pussy eagerly accepting everything he had to give. His abs were hard and tight and flexing, and when he pulled back she could see the thick root of his cock emerging from her sex and it turned her on even more.

Rocking her hips to meet his, she arched up from the bed.

Garth groaned, slowing his pace a moment before pressing on, his eyes barely open as he stared down at her. The muscles in his neck stood out, his shoulders working as he lifted up on his arms to press deeper still.

She locked her legs round his hips, and as she did he pressed against her clit, sending her into orbit. When her core spasmed, Garth joined her in release, groaning loudly as he did so.

When he reluctantly pulled free he looked beyond her.

She knew Jai was there, behind her on the bed, naked.

He'd lain alongside her back and when she wilted against him his hands outlined her body. He kissed her shoulder, his hand cupping her breast. When he trailed his fingers over her nut-hard nipple, she cried out.

"Oh, so sensitive now that Garth has battered you into the bed."

There was a low growl in his voice and he moved his hand over her body, stroking her everywhere. "It was hard to hang back, with all this loveliness here on your bed."

Garth seemed riveted. His chest rose and fell rapidly as he recovered from his climax. Faye reached out one hand to clasp his, using him as an anchor while Jai explored her body from behind.

She was so far gone, so racked with pleasure, that his touch drove her crazy. When he stroked her buttocks she automatically pushed back to meet him. He squeezed her flesh, still kissing the back of her neck, then he moved his hands between her thighs to embrace her swollen pussy.

"Oh, God!"

He stroked his fingers into her swollen, damp folds, playing her body like an instrument. Then came the swift glide of his sheathed cock into her sensitised sex.

"I'm going to die of pleasure!" It was almost too much, so soon after, but she was helpless in the face of it, unable to do anything but enjoy each thrust he gave her.

Garth looked on, watching her as her body rippled each time Jai entered her. He seemed glued to the image.

Faye could scarcely believe it. She was in heaven, her body rolling on the edge of orgasm. She shuddered.

"Easy now, nearly there now lover." He locked his hands on her hips, which kept her still from the waist down.

"Suck her breasts, like you did earlier," he instructed Garth.

"I want to feel you come," he added, whispering in her ear while he took shallow thrusts. "Let me feel you."

She tried to respond, but couldn't.

Garth shifted, kneeling next to the bed he leaned over to kiss and lick her breasts. Garth had kept hold of her hand, and she gripped it tightly. It was as if Garth's tongue and teeth on her tender flesh triggered her release and her core tightened, released, tightened again.

Jai murmured something incomprehensible at her back and his cock arched and jerked in orgasm—rubbing against the front wall of her sex—and set loose another bolt of pleasure. Hot fluid sluiced down her inner thighs and her entire groin and lower belly burned with the heat of her release.

Still he rode in and out of her, even after he came, which only served to draw out her climax until she felt faint with it and felt as if she'd have to be peeled off the bed.

By the time she could focus, Garth was kissing her palm.

"You look gorgeous," he whispered.

"I agree. You were made for this." Jai's cock slipped from her body and he leaned right over to kiss her mouth.

Where Garth was demanding with his kisses, Jai was more playful and seductive. She reached out with her free hand and threaded her fingers through his hair, marvelling at how it felt to have two men pleasuring her. It surpassed every fantasy she'd ever had.

"So, let me get this straight," Jai said, capturing her right on the edge, rolling her to her back, as if determined not to let her drift, "you've been looking for the right two guys to have a threesome with?"

"What, oh." Faye took a breath then laughed.

He had a faux quizzical glance on his face. He kept it light, in the aftermath.

"No, it wasn't quite like that." She was trapped in his arms, and she wriggled until she freed one hand then thumped his chest playfully.

"But you knew someone who'd had two men, and it made you curious?"

She turned her head on the pillow and looked at Garth.

When their eyes met he reached out and stroked her hair, as if he'd been waiting to touch her again. Something about his expression made her ache to touch him too.

"Yes, it made me curious. It's my sister, so I…um, hear a lot about it." She kept it to one sister for the time being. She didn't think it would be right to announce she felt like the odd one out because both her sisters were involved in three way relationships.

"Sister, huh. That explains it." Jai shifted onto his side, which left space for Garth to move closer to her other side and lay alongside her. "Your eyes, my dear, were everywhere… when you turned up here."

"You're a cheeky sort, aren't you," Faye said, but she laughed.

It could have got heavy there afterwards, but he made it seem like it was the most natural thing in the world for them to be lying in Garth's bed, three of them, talking about their first moments together. "My eyes are always everywhere. It's part of my natural curiosity about life, and the afterlife, and everything."

"You're still curious about the ghost, now?" Jai seemed surprised.

"What, you think I'd forgotten about my commission, just because you were both showing me such a good time?" She could give as good as she got with the teasing, but it served as a reminder. She quickly put out feelers. There was some paranormal activity in the house, but it was a remainder of what went before. She *had* forgotten—which even she could forgive herself for, given the circumstances—but Jai didn't need his ego boosted. Not right then.

"Besides, I might have been curious about having a threesome, but I never really thought it would happen. I assumed it would remain a fantasy, to be completely honest with you."

When she smiled at him, Garth shifted, unfurling his limbs as he took up the place that was there on the bed for him.

"I'm glad I got to be part of your fantasy." He looked at her as if he entranced.

Faye acted on instinct. Reaching up, she wrapped her hands around his head as she kissed him. His mouth, so firm and masculine, moved against hers as he returned her kiss with passion. With a possessive hand he drew her close to his chest, then moved it in small circular motions against her back, as if soothing her.

The man was big and gruff and competitive by nature, but he had a gentle side to him that made her feel cherished. Behind her she heard Jai plump a pillow as he shifted up the bed.

When she drew away from Garth and glanced back she saw that Jai had propped himself up and was happily observing.

"Don't let me interrupt," he said, and waved his hand encouragingly.

Faye felt her face heat, but it didn't matter. The self-consciousness she felt only seemed to make it better—wilder and kinkier. She had begun to discover her exhibitionist streak.

Garth's eyes were darkening. Against her thigh his cock was getting hard. "Can you go another round?"

Laughing softly, she nodded. When she lay on her back, Garth climbed over her, easing her legs apart to lie between them.

"I may die of ecstasy," she added.

"I'm so glad you've got a twelve pack of condoms," Jai commented at her side, with irony. "It looks as if it's going to be long night."

Chapter Five

Faye stirred in her sleep. The atmosphere changing in the house had disturbed her. Once she felt that, it quickly pulled her out of her doze. Lifting her head from the pillow she blinked and looked around. The presence of a man either side of her made her inhale sharply, the events of the evening quickly running through her mind.

Faye savoured their masculine bodies, marvelling at how that made her afterglow that much more vibrant. Then a wave of tension rippled through the atmosphere from the direction of the staircase beyond. The men slumbered on. Was the ghost on the prowl? She knew she would have to pursue it, even though she wanted to stay right where she was.

With extreme care she extracted herself from the tangle of arms and legs and manoeuvred down the bed. Picking up an abandoned shirt on the way, she pulled it on to cover her nakedness, then made her way toward the apparition who unwittingly sent out psychic information on the staircase outside. Garth had said the ghost favoured the downstairs, especially the kitchen. Perhaps curiosity had drawn her closer.

Was there more than one resident ghost? The question occurred to her as Faye crept toward the landing outside Garth's flat. Whoever it was, she willed the spirit not to depart. At the doorway she watched and waited, but she felt pretty sure there was only one spirit out there, the woman she'd seen earlier. Braving herself for whatever she would face, she stepped out on to the gloomy landing and closed the door behind her.

Walking quickly down the stairs, she isolated herself with the ghostly presence that materialised on the landing below.

The woman backed into a corner and stared fixedly at Faye. "You can see me?"

Her reed-thin voice was barely audible.

Faye nodded. "I have the ability. My name is Faye."

She hoped the woman would reveal her name, or some other identifying detail that would help in the hunt for information. Instead she looked beyond her and up the stairs into Garth's private space.

As Faye became accustomed to the gloom she saw that a look of dismay was apparent in the ghost's expression. When she looked back at Faye she frowned.

Great, a jealous ghost. "Are you happy that people live here again?"

"I was."

Oh dear. "I'm only a visitor here. I'll be gone soon. Please tell me your name."

The spirit looked a smidge less irritated, but she was definitely rather possessive about the two men. "Maud, Maud Radisson."

Faye took a step closer and stretched out her fingers, turning her palms toward the spirit, opening herself to any contained memories and emotions that might be carried with her.

The woman, Maud, eyed her warily.

"Why do you linger here?"

The spirit looked confused. She shook her head at Faye.

"Tell me," Faye encouraged, "I can help you."

Again Maud shook her head. "No one can help me."

"Well no, not if you snap at them like that they won't."

Maud's lips thinned and she folded her arms over her chest.

Back to aggression and being defensive. Nevertheless, Faye had the feeling she was annoyed with herself most of all. "Don't you want to talk?"

Faye shrugged and began to turn away.

"Look here," Maud blurted, halting Faye's footsteps. "No one else who's come to this house has been able to see me. There was no one for me to communicate with until you came."

Faye turned around. "You're saying you're a bit rusty and I should ignore your rather blunt remarks and your jealousy?"

Maud pursed her lips, but nodded. "Yes. Sorry."

The apology was grudgingly given, but it was also obvious she didn't want to give up the chance to converse with someone who could see her.

"Did many people come before? I heard the house was empty for a long time."

"Oh yes, it was, officially. But still people came. For a while three people lived here." Her expression immediately began to lift as she spoke. "Squatters, that's what they called themselves. They couldn't see me though." She said it with a weary resignation, as if she still couldn't quite believe it, after all these years. "Then one morning the coppers came and broke through the door and forced them to leave."

"I didn't particularly like them, always talking politics they were, but I missed them when they were gone." She gave a self-deprecatory laugh. "Surprised myself there."

"Someone to watch?"

Maud nodded. "Occasionally people would barge in here just to look at the place, peeling off the plaster on the walls and poking things in the floorboards." She looked annoyed by that. Her connection to the house was deep.

"Surveyors perhaps," Faye suggested.

Maud observed Faye with wary curiosity, as if she wasn't quite sure what a surveyor was but didn't want to ask. "For a long time it seemed as if no one would ever live here again and the building would just rot away…like me."

"You must have been pleased when Garth and Jai bought the place?"

"I like them, and it was fun to watch the builders while they were working. Although I'm not sure about some of the things they did here."

Faye cast her mind back to where she knew about the 1960s and realised how different this must look to Maud. "Some of the things they've done here are because they are architects. They want to make an impression."

"Is that why they put the glass wall in?" Maud seemed generally intrigued.

"Yes, it's so that people who are sitting in the waiting room can see where the work goes and get a feel for the kind of ideas they have, with those scale models of buildings."

It felt odd informing Maud, a resident, about the house usage, but Faye had the feeling Maud appreciated it. It also made Maud relax, which would hopefully lead to a deeper discussion. Faye had an agenda. She needed to know what kept Maud here.

"Back in my time all of that would have been hidden. Things were changing, but mostly no one knew how stuff was made."

"What year was it, when your life ended?"

Maud became tense. She glanced away, and for several moments an awkward silence filled the atmosphere. "It's all a bit of a blur, but I think maybe it was early in 1965. It was winter."

Faye wasn't sure if she should push any further, but Maud stared at her, an expectant, challenging look in her eyes, and the question hung in the air between them.

"Maud, did you die here in the house?"

Maud's face went blank.

"Maud?"

Inside a heartbeat, her spirit faded and was gone.

"Damn and blast. I asked too soon." She glanced around the landing and back at the spot where Maud had stood. "Sorry, love. I shouldn't have asked you that."

Maud would come back, she told herself. Meanwhile, she could find out herself how Maud had died by doing little bit more digging. Now that she knew her name, she had a start.

She stepped over to the place where Maud had stood in order to engage with her residual psychic aura, forming a connection with her before it wisped away on the night air.

Then she glanced at the light at the landing window. It was near dawn. In a few hours, the offices of the registrar of birth and death would be open and she would get started. Meanwhile, good progress had been made in the communication stakes, and hopefully Maud would share more soon.

"Her name is Maud." Faye hesitated, unsure if the news about Maud's attraction to the two men would cause even more tension between them. "She's developed quite a fondness for you and seemed quite put out by my presence."

Jai laughed softly. "Are you saying she doesn't like having other women around?"

"Maybe. I'm not sure yet." She munched on a second croissant. Jai had brought them breakfast in bed.

"I have an ex who was like that," Jai added. "Couldn't stand it when another woman tried to speak to me."

"Do you blame her," Garth mumbled in between sipping his coffee.

"I think she'll get used to it," Faye clarified. "At least she told me her name, so she's starting to communicate. It was only when I asked about her attachment to this place that she backed off. I think it would really help to get out there and find out a bit more about Maud."

Garth looked puzzled. "You can do that?"

"Local council records, registrar's office, library, that sort of thing. A bit more specific digging than I can do on the Internet."

Jai stretched and yawn. "I'll come with you, sounds intriguing. What time does this place open?"

"That's a point, look at the time." Garth sprang into action, leaping out of the bed like an Olympic athlete.

Faye watched, agog with interest at his naked body in action.

Garth looked back at Jai, who still lazed on the bed with his arms behind his head. "We're due at Parkinson's site in half an hour. He wants to go over the plans today." He opened the wardrobe and reached for a hanger, pulling out a white linen shirt. "You do remember, don't you?"

Faye watched, fascinated by the way these two functioned as friends and colleagues. Jai was unperturbed. He looked like a lazy lion awakening, his roving gaze on what was to be had. When he looked her way she saw that hungry look in his eyes that indicated he wasn't thinking about breakfast.

"In that case, I'm going to head to the registrar's office while you're out, see what I can find out about our friend Maud.

Jai continued to convince Garth of his plans. "You'll be at the site most of the day. You can handle it. I have faith in you. I'll bring Faye over when we're done."

Faye wondered if he'd added that last as a sweetener. Garth didn't look altogether sweetened, but he let it go.

"Not what you were expecting?"

Faye shook her head and glanced back at the registrar's office with a thoughtful expression.

She really did investigate, Jai decided. When Garth had shown him her ad, he thought she might be a bit of a nutter, or a clever con on the take, but she really had engaged with the spirit in the building and the whole history of events.

"Where to next?"

"The local library. We can look at the newspapers on microfiche."

Faye stayed quiet on the journey, as if deep in thought.

Once they got to the library and she requested the relevant newspaper microfiches, Jai found them side-by-side readers and offered to help.

They began to scan the pages, reading through newspapers from the time of Maud's death.

"You look as if you're familiar with these machines?" Faye commented as she worked through the data.

"Yes, we sometimes have to use them to look at older foundation plans. Used them a lot as students of course."

"That's when you met Garth, as students?"

"Uh huh. We had to work on a project together and I've been stuck with him ever since." He flashed her a grin.

He liked her smile and she showed it to him then.

"Funnily enough, the task we had to do together was specifically designed to show students how a project can benefit from having different interpretations, different minds thinking through the problems together."

Faye stopped what she was doing for a moment and looked at him thoughtfully. When she returned to her microfiche she gasped and pointed at the screen. "I think I found something."

She scanned up and down the piece. "It's a very small article, but it mentions the death of a woman who worked locally. It describes the accident and says that she was single and worked as a cook in a local business."

She sat back in her chair.

"Useful?"

"I hope so. It means I can ask more leading questions the next time she appears." She rose to her feet, apparently enthused by what she'd found out.

Jai admired that quality about her. And many others.

After they'd returned the microfiches they made their way back to the car. He held the passenger door open for her and watched as she got in. She moved like a dancer, somehow elegant and graceful even in her bohemian gear, as if she'd done ballet or something. Whatever, it appealed to him. And to Garth. Yes, being around Faye had revealed a side of Garth he hadn't seen before, one that his old friend had previously denied.

He got into the driver's seat and put the key in the ignition, then paused. It was past midday, but he knew Garth would be handling things at the site. Faye looked as if she needed to talk.

Faye had her head back against the head rest and seemed deep in thought.

"What are you thinking?"

"Well, we now know the cause of death. It was a car accident on an icy road. No suspicious circumstances. Not that the police recorded, at any rate."

"What did you think it might be?"

She shrugged and turned to look at him. "Sadly, several cases I've encountered have been suicides, and that's what held them to our world."

Jai didn't have an answer to that, mostly because he could see that she carried some of the sadness she'd experienced.

As if she grew aware of him studying her, she focused. "Maud's was a tragic death but it was an accident. Mind you, I'm glad I don't have to tell Garth that someone died in dubious circumstances in his house."

"No, that is good news. Garth really doesn't need any more reasons to take himself seriously."

"Yes, I can see you are dedicated to helping lighten him up." The warmth in her smile made Jai doubly aware of how much he liked her.

"I like the guy, I figured out I could help him out with that."

Her eyes twinkled. "In for the long haul, huh?"

She was very astute, and he felt the humour of the moment passing between them as she locked gazes with him.

"It does seem to have become a life cause." He shifted in his seat and turned to face her properly. "It was good to see him loosening up a bit last night. Everybody needs a little bit of kinky sex in their lives."

Recognition flickered in her eyes. "How kinky do you like to get?"

Trailing his fingers along her thigh, he looked directly into her eyes a bit longer.

Faye's lips parted and her eyes darkened. She was such a sensual, responsive woman.

"I'm all for experimentation, going with the flow when life presents intriguing opportunities. Last night was good. Garth was turned on, even when he wasn't getting in on the act." He winked at her. "He wouldn't admit it though."

"And you?"

"Of course, I love watching sex." He eased his fingers over the curve of her thigh and between her legs. "I enjoy experimenting, capturing the moment. Life is short, after all."

Her eyes widened and she nodded down at his roving hand. "This is what you mean by going with the flow?"

"You're a very attractive woman, and you haven't slapped my wrist…you haven't crossed your legs and crushed my hand…yet." He gave her his cheekiest grin. "I figure you're going with the flow, as am I."

He moved his hand higher and cupped her pussy through her underwear. Then he reached in for a kiss.

She returned his kiss immediately and looped her hands around his neck as if she'd been waiting for it. Her hips moved, and he could feel the heat of her pussy in his hand.

When they drew apart a man walked close by the front of the car and Faye clasped Jai's hand, arresting it. When the man went to a car two along the row Faye moved his hand higher, so that it covered her breast.

"You see, I knew you were a playful type." Even through her top and bra he could feel her nipple.

"So that's what you liked about me, huh," she breathed. "Open minded, and willing to go with the flow?"

He moved his hand, holding his palm flat against the hard bump of her nipple, gently clasping the curve of her breast. He nodded. "That and your sexy eyes."

"You're the one with the sexy eyes." She laughed softly, lifted his hand from her breast and kissed it in the palm, sending his nerve endings crazy. When he let it free, she reached down and pulled her skirt a little higher, wriggling her hips to assist, revealing the triangle of fabric over her pussy. Mischief sparkled in her eyes. "Is that what you were looking for?"

Jai nodded. His cock hardened. He reached in to kiss her neck. She smelt of musk, of woman and desire. When he returned his hand to her pussy she kissed him again, holding his face in her hands as her tongue teased against his.

He traced his fingers along the insides of her thighs and noticed that she pressed her head back against the headrest when he dipped his fingers down one side of her panties to touch her pussy.

She moaned, gasped against his mouth, trembling.

He moved his fingers deeper. Her cunt felt hot and slippery, and when he moved his fingers in and out her flesh closed around them, clasping them in a way that made him wish it was his cock instead.

Drawing back, he studied her. Her eyelids lowered and she looked deliciously aroused, making his cock pound. He ignored it. He wanted to concentrate on her and learn what she liked. Shifting his hand he moved his thumb over the bump of her clit.

"Oh, oh, oh…" She caught her bottom lip between her teeth, her fingers clutching at his shirt sleeve while she shuddered in release.

Her body rolled closer to his and she put her forehead on his shoulder while uttering a muffled moan into his shirt. Smiling to himself, he stroked his fingers around the mouth of her cunt before dipping inside again. When she lifted her head from his shoulder to look at him, Jai was captured by her expression. Her cheeks were flushed, her lips dark and parted as she panted for breath.

He moved his free hand to stroke her jaw.
She was lush and playful, sophisticated and wild.
He liked her. He liked her a lot.

Chapter Six

The site Garth were worked was impressive—a huge, half-built glass-covered building that twisted skyward. Faye stared up at it when they climbed out of the car in the small, muddy car park at the site. "Well, this is a new experience for me. I've never been inside a new building while it's under construction."

"Believe it or not this place is over five years old." Jai led her on to a makeshift pathway made of sheets of board that were only marginally less muddy than the surrounding area. "It was a victim of the recession. The original developer went bust and the build got put on hold. Thankfully a new developer has taken it on board and he's hired us to take a look at the space again, to advise him how it might be developed differently to maximise take-up once it's finished."

Jai led the way and picked up two hard hats from a shelving unit inside the door. He insisted she put one on.

"Suits you," he commented.

"Yeah right." She noticed he looked right at home in his.

Inside the core of the building she spied Garth. He looked even more gorgeous than he had that morning when he flung on his smart suit, even though the jacket was currently nowhere to be seen. His shirt was still done up neatly, as was the tie, but his sleeves were rolled up revealing his strong forearms. The contrast of dapper outfit and brawn suited him. Faye watched as he talked to the group of builders and pointed around the inside of the building with his pen, noting the easy camaraderie he had with the men. "He enjoys his work?"

"Oh yes," Jai responded, "he's a natural born architect, great vision when it comes to a project like this."

Faye noticed a subtle note of pride in Jai's voice. They had a deep bond, these two. At first she'd seen the competitive edge—mostly good hearted—but the more time she spent around them she learned that there was much more to their friendship. "Is he a better architect than you?"

Jai looked at her, clearly amused by the question. "Of course he is. He needs me though, because he doesn't have the self-belief he should have."

"You push him forward?"

Jai nodded.

Just then Garth caught sight of them standing nearby. He paused for a moment and nodded their way—staring across at them with a thoughtful expression—then wound up his conversation with the builders. Putting his documents down on the table, he headed over.

"You missed the client," he said to Jai.

"I'll deal with him next time, to make up to you."

Faye noticed that Jai grinned at him. Garth nodded, then looked at them both with curiosity. She was about to tell him what they'd found out about Maud when he spoke.

"You two got it on, didn't you?"

"My, my, what a suspicious and dirty mind you have," Jai teased.

"You bloody well did though, didn't you?"

Faye was surprised.

Jai seemed to enjoy the situation. "Don't worry, we restrained our natural urges, so you didn't miss too much."

Only the best orgasm I've ever had in a car, Faye thought to herself, but kept her lip buttoned. Should she feel guilty about what had happened? She wasn't quite sure. It was all too new. Garth, however, seemed as much fascinated as he did suspicious.

Erotic tension rose between the three of them, fast and furious, palpable and intoxicating.

Jai, meanwhile, seemed intent on telling Garth the details. "Okay, I confess it was my fault. I couldn't resist. I gave Faye a little fondle in my car."

"A little fondle?" Garth really did want all the details.

Faye swayed on her heels. He'd wanted to be part of it, she realised. That notion turned her on immensely.

Garth looked at her with possessive eyes while Jai continued to describe what had gone on.

Faye's breathing altered because she suddenly became aware just how aroused Garth was. Glancing down then quickly away, she took in the sight of the bulge at his groin. Those expensive trousers of his were well and truly packed. With an effort she stared across at a builder who was measuring some sort of girder. It didn't help. The nagging ache at her centre reminded her that she had two eager men close at hand, one who was currently looking at her as if he was about to tear her clothes off right here in full view of any workmen who might look their way.

"Perhaps we should continue this conversation elsewhere," she suggested, and her voice wavered.

"You read my mind." Garth put his arm around the back of her shoulders and led her quickly toward a doorway behind her.

She practically had to run to keep up with him, and when she glanced back she saw Jai followed behind them. He flickered an eyebrow at her, letting her know that he'd triggered this deliberately. That made her arousal levels soar. Jai's provocative sexual manoeuvres made her feel heady and reckless.

"This way." Garth drew her into a stairwell and down, as if toward the basement. Their footsteps echoed up the unfinished staircases above, the raw state of the surroundings making the sound of their feet even more hollow and echo-filled than they would have been in a finished unit.

Garth held her hand and darted down the steps to where they ended in the basement. Plastic wrapped stacks of floor tiles cluttered the place. There he backed her into a gloomy corner underneath the stairs. He tugged off his hard hat, dropped it to the floor and put his hands on her hips, clutching at her dress. For the second time that day, her skirt rode up around her hips in an almost-public place.

"I want to touch you." His voice was husky with desire.

Faye lifted her chin, challenging him. "Go ahead, touch me."

He lifted off her hard hat, casting it aside. It rolled across the floor coming to a halt next to his. Weaving his fingers through her loosened hair, he kissed her. Her lips parted readily, welcoming the brusque contact. The passion she felt in him washed over.

She flattened her hands to the wall behind her and rocked her hips against him, offering herself, urging him on silently with her eyes.

His fingers plucked at the fabric, pulling it away from her mons. The band tightened and she felt the cold air on her intimate places as he shoved her undies down her thighs. She wriggled to assist, loving that he made her feel so brazen when her knickers fell around her ankles. Lifting one foot, she freed one leg.

His hand immediately went to her buttock, cupping it, encouraging her to lift her leg high against his side. The other hand stroked into her wet warmth, his fingers opening her up.

"You're so hot there."

"You're turning me on, that's why." She nodded down at his bulging zipper.

With his thumb up in her crease he applied pressure to her clit and pushed two fingers inside her.

Her head went back against the wall and she rode his fingers, the hard intrusion making her wild.

Jai stood at the bottom of the staircase, one hand on the railing, and occasionally glanced away from them and up the stairs. He watched out in case anyone else came down.

The thought that someone might arrive made her wilder still, her whole body shunting. Garth continued to thrust his fingers in and out of her, but she wanted more. She clasped his erection through his trousers.

He cursed beneath his breath. "Be careful."

She fumbled for the zipper. "Have you got a condom?"

He glanced back over his shoulder. "Jai?"

Jai shoved his hand into his pocket and pulled out the required item. He handed over the packet. "Just as well one of us was prepared."

"Hey, I don't have to be, because you always are." Garth smiled at Faye. Turning the condom packet in his fingers he gazed into her eyes. "Are you sure? You've got me in a state, but we can still stop this."

Even though he'd paused, the barely withheld thrust of his body against hers thrilled her. "You're always so right and proper…just before you let rip."

Jai laughed aloud at her comment.

It was crazy. She knew she was egging him on. One glance over his shoulder assured her that Jai enjoyed the show, and Garth was really loosening up. She instinctively knew this wasn't the sort of thing that he normally did, and nor did she. She didn't want to stop now, and neither did he.

"Please, Faye. Say no quickly if you don't want to go ahead with this, because it's getting more and more difficult for me to pull back." His voice was akin to a growl.

"Fuck me, please." She squeezed her hand over his bulging zipper. In the background she caught sight of Jai's wicked smile. "In the car, earlier, Jai just teased me," she said, channelling Jai's mood. "He got me hot and ready for you, and now I need you to give it to me…hard."

Garth's eyes flashed with triumph. "Oh, I will."

While Garth rolled the condom over his erection, she attempted to stabilise her breathing and take stock of this crazy situation. Jai had rested his elbow on the bottom of the railing on the staircase, eyes twinkling as he observed the pair of them. He winked at Faye when she looked his way. She pursed her mouth at him in a silent kiss. Garth wasn't taking himself too seriously at the moment that was for sure.

Once he'd donned the condom, she wrapped her arms around his neck and he lifted her with his hands under her buttocks. She wrapped her legs around his hips and crossed her ankles behind him

His cock nudged against her, then slipped inside.

Garth worked quickly, thrusting deep and hard, riding her against the wall. Faye revelled in it. Clutching his shoulders, she angled her body into his, her shoulders pivoting against the wall at her back.

The sound of men's voices shouting to one another and laughter echoed down the stairs from above. "Oh, God, don't let them come down here, please."

She blurted it out, but somehow the threat of discovery made her even hornier, and her vision blurred at the intensity. She was right on the edge, and she didn't want to stop now. Clasping on his erection with her inner muscles, she locked eyes with him and nodded her head.

"Oh yes," Garth whispered, and she could see he reckoned with his self-control. His spoke through gritted teeth then glanced back over his shoulder. "Jai?"

Before he had a chance to say anything else, Jai was on the case. "I'll derail them if they intend coming down here." He turned away. There was reluctance in his steps, but he hastened upwards to create a distraction.

Faye's eyes rolled as she realised he'd stopped the men right on the floor above. She shook her head at Garth, but he was not about to be stopped. He drove in and out like a machine, and she was so slippery that he rode right up against each and every part of her, crushing against her cervix.

"Garth," she whispered desperately, fingers digging into his shoulders.

She nodded at him. His cock was deep, pushing up against the neck of her womb. He rolled his hips from side to side and she came with a sudden rush of sensation, her clit tingling wildly, her groin awash with heavy heat. He held her tight while she came, protecting her.

For a moment she lost contact with the surroundings then she was back there, because Garth's cock was jerking in release. His eyes closed and she saw extreme effort in his expression, as if he struggled to stay quiet. In the raw core of the building, while men's voices echoed above, Garth gave her a kiss which was so deep and possessive, that she clung to him gratefully, mourning the loss as he slid from her body and lowered her gently to her feet.

Quickly he rearranged himself and zipped up his fly then he was all about assisting her, retrieving her panties from the floor he helped her into them as she swayed unsteadily.

Shaky after her intense climax and dizzy with the insanity of the moment, Faye had to suppress a giggle. "You're crazy," she whispered to him.

As he straightened up he replied. "Only where you're concerned, believe me."

He collected their hard hats and once they had them back on he nodded his head upwards. "Ready?"

Faye smoothed her dress over her hips with her free hand, took a deep breath and nodded.

Chapter Seven

"Oh my God, they knew." Faye couldn't stop giggling as the three of them made their way back to Jai's car.

The men thought it was pretty amusing too, especially Jai. "They didn't know for sure, but they had their suspicions. This will do wonders for your reputation stud."

Garth shook his head, but Faye could see he secretly enjoyed it.

"The best bit," Jai continued, "was when you said you'd been showing the lady around. You do realise that only drew attention to the fact that you'd come from a gloomy dead-end corridor."

"If I could be practical for a moment," Garth interrupted, once they were inside the car, "let's stop at the deli, I'll cook tonight."

"No, let's go out to eat," Faye said, "if that's okay. My treat, since you've been looking after me so well. I'd just like to gather my thoughts about your house and its guest before we head back. Time out, as it were."

"As long as you don't want time out from us," Jai commented.

"No way." That was the last thing she wanted.

In reality she had to think about Maud without wondering if Maud was watching them and listening. She also felt a little guilty that she hadn't spent more time working on Maud. Everything that had happened with Jai and Garth was hot and alive and a dream come true, but it wasn't enabling her to get stuck in to her job and figure out Maud in the way she really needed—resolving her limbo state between two worlds.

Jai suggested Indian food and Garth heartily agreed. As they crossed London they chatted about the building site and their joint vision for the project. Once they got to the restaurant she realised that Jai had suggested somewhere they knew well. The floor manager waved as soon as they entered the place.

Jai ordered them a selection of dishes to try, not waiting for them to check the menu. It was obvious he was very familiar with the place.

"You can trust him on this score," Garth assured her.

When the food arrived Garth dipped into everything, eating heartily. Faye tasted three dishes and couldn't get any further because she discovered a delicately spiced fish curry that sent her taste buds to heaven and back. "Oh my God, my mouth is having an orgasm."

Jai nodded. "It's good food."

Jai kept getting up and walking into the kitchens, and chatting to the waiters.

"I take it they know him here," Faye asked.

"Rajit, the owner, is Jai's second or third cousin. We come here all the time and Jai wanders around chatting to people, like some sort of social butterfly." Garth looked quite content to have her to himself for a few minutes. In fact he looked more content than she'd seen him since she'd met him, twenty-four hours before.

Was it only 24 hours, she wondered. So much had happened. She felt as if she'd boarded a high-speed train and her whole life had shifted to fast forward, but in a good way.

"He's a bit of a free spirit, isn't he?" Faye nodded her head in Jai's direction. He'd emerged from the kitchen and stood in the doorway to the service area, apparently still engaged in a boisterous conversation.

"You could call it that. If it wasn't for me, he'd have no sense of responsibility whatsoever."

Faye repressed a smile. Both men believed that they were supporting the other in some crucial way. She couldn't resist teasing him about it. "You're like an old married couple, muddling through together."

"Well, I suppose that's one way of looking at it." Garth looked startled by her remark.

As they chatted on Faye manoeuvred the conversation back to the subject of Maud. "We found out Maud's birth and death day. She died in a car accident, ice on the road. About two streets away from your house."

"That's just so hard to imagine." Garth seemed nonplussed by the information. "It's difficult to put it all into perspective, having felt her presence there now."

"I'm getting a bit more used to it myself, now that I'm investigating things like this, but I know what you mean. It seems like we shouldn't be able to talk about her death the way we can." She picked up the Asian beer Jai had ordered for them and sipped. "It's going to take a bit more work to find out why she's attached to the house. That's what we need to know. I need to think about how I'm going to question her when I encounter her again."

Garth nodded, but looked as if he was thinking about something else entirely. He looked deep into her eyes, and his fork resting on his plate as if forgotten.

"I sense your thoughts are elsewhere," Faye teased.

"As odd as it is dealing with a paranormal presence, I'm glad that my unusual house guest problem has brought you into my life."

Faye sat back in her chair and gazed at him across the table, deeply pleased by his comment and the look on his face as he said it. "I must admit, it's been quite an adventure."

Something in his expression shifted and grew more intense.

Faye felt he was about to say something else, but Jai rejoined them.

"Enjoying the food?"

"Absolutely, it's the best I've ever had."

Jai grinned at her comment.

"Garth tells me you're related to the owner."

"And to the kitchen manager. It means I'll never starve." He waved back to the kitchens, where she noticed a young man in whites had stuck his head out and looked their way, apparently trying to catch sight of Jai's female guest.

"One of his more useful attributes," Garth commented.

As the conversation evolved, Faye felt blessed. Never before had her work brought her into contact with a man she'd been instantly attracted to, and now there were two.

Her practical nature demanded she organise her time to make the most of it though, so she took the bull by the horns. "I don't think we should have sex."

She waited until both of them gave her their attention. She didn't have to wait long.

Garth looked at her in dismay.

Jai shook his head in objection.

"At your place, tonight," she added, laughing softly. "I need to focus on the ghost tonight. You two are pulling my attention away."

Jai lifted his hands. "What the hell, Garth. Have you been distracting the lady from her work?"

Garth smiled at that.

"Now that I know a little bit about Maud, I feel I can draw her into conversation. I don't need a lot of sleep, but if I take a short nap this evening then I can stay awake tonight and wait around in her favourite places, the areas she shows up. If I'm there, she's more likely to come out."

"A magnet to ghosts as well as to mere mortal men, hmm?" Jai said, ever the charmer.

"Stop it." She felt embarrassed by that. "That's not what I meant. Anyway, I need to go home to change my clothes so I can grab a nap then."

"You should pack a weekend bag and stay over," Jai suggested.

Garth quickly added his encouragement. "Bring whatever you need. You might as well be comfortable at my place while you're um, on the job."

"You should have brought your stuff to begin with," Jai added.

"I didn't know I was going to get such convivial hosts then, did I?"

Garth reached across the table and caressed her hand. "Why don't we escort you to your place, then we can tuck you in for your nap."

"Can you afford the time?"

Garth nodded quickly. "Hell yes, anything else can wait."

Jai agreed. "I've already cancelled my squash game for tomorrow morning so I'll be on hand for anything you might need."

Garth arched his eyebrows at his cohort but he didn't say anything.

"Well, if you're sure. Actually, I'd love to get a photo of you two in my flat." That way she'd always have it to remember. As the thought occurred to her, she realised how sad she'd be to say goodbye to them, after the job was done. It quelled her bubbly mood for a moment.

"I've got a confession," she added quickly. It was something that had been playing on her mind and she needed to get it out in the open. "When I said it was my sister who is in a three-way relationship, that wasn't quite the whole story."

She had their full attention.

"I have two older sisters, and they are both in a ménage à trois relationship." Her face heated, because it shone a spotlight on her motives.

"No wonder you were curious." Jai's eyes glinted. He seemed intrigued.

Garth studied her thoughtfully. "That's why you wanted to meet two men who were willing, because they had?"

"Well, it wasn't quite like that. I was curious about it, and I suppose that made me open to it. To be honest I never thought I'd have the opportunity."

Jai shrugged. "It's a common enough fantasy."

She smiled his way. She'd felt a little awkward making her confession, but it had to come out or she might trip herself up by saying something about it at the wrong time. Jai had a knack of diffusing tension, making everything seem as if it wasn't a big deal.

"You must have a lot of birthdays to remember, with all those other halves," Jai added.

She chuckled. "Christmas was a bit of a nightmare, I have to say. It's hard enough finding a good gift for men anyway without having to double it up all the time."

Garth still looked thoughtful. "I feel like the odd one out, you both have large families."

Faye noticed that he focused on the family aspect, not the unusual long-term relationships she'd mentioned. Perhaps that was easier for him. "You're an only child?"

"I have an older sister but she's worked in Spain since she left Uni, so we don't hook up as a family as often as we should."

As the conversation moved on to their upbringings Faye began to learn more about her two lovers. How lucky she'd been, to experience this. But she'd got so much more than her fantasy made real. It wasn't just the sexual experimentation, it was being around them. The way they were together tickled her, and she enjoyed their company, fast growing to care about them on another level.

Pull back, she warned herself. Twenty-four hours was too soon to feel this way. But she couldn't help it. She felt gloriously happy, dazzled by her good fortune, and eager to experiment some more.

Chapter Eight

"Oh yes, this is good." Jai crossed to Faye's bed, turned around and threw himself back on it, arms outstretched. "This is *way* more comfortable than your bed, Garth." He picked up the cuddly lion she had sitting on the spare pillow and began to toss it up and down in his hands.

Faye couldn't withhold her smile. "You look quite at home there, which makes me doubt my ability to get a proper nap in."

Jai propped himself on one elbow and grinned.

Garth rubbed her shoulder affectionately. "Don't worry. I'll make sure you get plenty of rest before tonight, even if I have to take him out kicking and screaming."

"Now that I'd like to see." Faye felt intoxicated by their presence. Somehow having them in her tiny little flat, her private space, felt like she would keep part of them there. It was a memory to cherish.

"This man can make himself comfortable in any bed," Garth continued. "It's in his personality to nest wherever he happens to be."

"Do you even have your own bed?" Faye asked.

Garth shook his head at his friend. "You wouldn't think so would you?"

Jai shrugged with one shoulder.

Faye's curiosity had been baited. "Where is your bed? You haven't mentioned where you live."

Garth gave a wry laugh then folded his arms over his chest. He didn't say anything, but looked at Jai expectantly. When Jai didn't offer any more information, Garth responded for him. "Jai still lives with his family. Thirty-two years old and he still hasn't got his own place."

Jai gestured with his free hand, still holding on to the cuddly toy with the other one. "I'm never at home, what's the point?"

"There's a weird sort of logic there, but maybe if you had your own place you'd spend more time in it."

"Maybe, but where's the fun in that?" That wickedly suggestive look of his had returned and it made Faye brim with reciprocal energy. There was something vital about Jai—something eternally elusive too—but where he chose to spend his time meant fun for those who were there. Was that why these two worked so well together—because Garth needed Jai, and Jai always had a good cause in making Garth have fun?

Meanwhile, Garth seemed to love the fact Jai was being exposed. "I offered him the floor below mine at the house. It's all but empty at the moment and he's invested in the place, so he has the right. But no. That would be too much responsibility for him."

"What do I need with responsibility? That's what you're for."

It tickled Faye because it was so obviously an illusion. If he'd invested, he already had the responsibility. He just wasn't reaping the same reward Garth was when it came to personal space. "Wherever you lay your hat, that's your home?"

Jai nodded. "The lady really is psychic."

"You haven't decided where to lay your hat yet, that's what it is."

"Maybe." He seemed pleased that she was so attuned to him.

"She's got your card marked," Garth said.

Jai's smile grew.

For some reason Faye felt a bit giddy. "I have to get a photo of you both, on my bed."

"Really?" Garth looked confused.

"Call it a souvenir." She darted off to find her bag. While she rifled through her bag in the hallway she heard them laughing. Jai was winding Garth up, by the sounds of it. He seemed to do that a lot. This time it was a commentary about posing for sexy photographs on a woman's bed with another man.

When she located her phone she rejoined them. Standing at the end of the bed, she switched it to camera mode and looked at them on the screen. Jai still reclined on the bed. Garth was sitting on the edge of it rather gingerly.

She laughed. "Try to look as if you've been enjoying an exciting three-way in my bed, why don't you."

Garth gave her a reprimanding glance. "That would be so much easier if we had just done that." He looked her up and down very deliberately.

Pleasure bubbled up inside her.

"Now you're talking." Jai put the cuddly toy aside and opened his arms to her.

So much for napping. Maybe she should have said no to them escorting her home for a rest. "Oh, come on, I want the picture."

Garth held up his hands and shifted to lie out alongside Jai.

Jai put the cuddly toy between them and made a big show of kissing it.

Laughing, Faye grabbed the shot.

Jai leapt to his feet. "You get on the bed for the next one. Wait, has your camera got a time delay?"

"Yup." Faye pointed it out as she handed it over.

"In that case we can all be in the photo. You get on the bed and I'll set it up." He arranged the camera on the dresser opposite the bed, then darted back and joined them.

They posed for the photo. The camera clicked and Jai got up again. "Wait there. I'll see how it came out."

While he checked out the camera, Garth moved up against Faye's side. "He's right. Your bed is more comfortable than mine."

"You reckon?" When she turned to look at him, he kissed her.

Caught unawares, she hesitated. Then melted. It was the affect he had on her. Garth was hesitant at first, then full-on.

By the time they drew apart, Jai had lifted her phone from its perch and studied it. "You did know this can record video, right?"

"Um, yes. I haven't used it though. I've only had it since Christmas."

Jai's slow, suggestive smile made her realise what he was getting at.

"You really ought to test it out," he said. "Make a home movie."

Her pulse beat more erratically. "You don't mean what I think you mean?"

"Why not? You wanted a souvenir."

An erotic home movie? She exchanged looks with Garth but neither of them verbalised their thoughts. She had the feeling he was as surprised as she was. Was he as curious as she was, too? It was something that she'd never considered before, but the idea seemed so hot it sent her spinning. Could she face up to a recording of herself in action, with not one but two lovers? As she thought about it, she realised just how hot a keepsake it would be. Performing while a camera recorded them would take some nerve, but to get a souvenir like that she was willing to push herself to a new level of brazenness.

Jai was busy studying the settings on her phone.

"Do you want to give it a go?" Garth's voice drew her attention back. The expression in his eyes was caring and sincere as he queried her, but the set of his mouth gave away how turned on he was by the idea of it. His lips were tight, erotic tension oozing from him as he held himself in check awaiting her consent.

"You are so adorable," she whispered, smiling.

He pulled back and looked at her. "I am?"

"Yes, you are so gentlemanly."

"I don't feel very gentlemanly right now." He drew her hand to his fly.

Faye inhaled when she felt how hard he was. His penis strained against the fabric of his trousers. Her hand closed around his rock hard erection and her core clenched, instantly craving it there, where it belonged.

"Are you attempting to seduce our woman?" Jai asked, hardly breaking with the job he had in hand to quiz Garth.

Garth nodded. "You better believe it."

Jai put the camera back on the dresser and leaned over to check the screen before he rejoined them. Then he stood at the end of the bed with his hands on his hips. "Tell me, Milady, what sort of souvenir are you after?"

He had taken control of the situation. But didn't he always? It occurred to her that that was exactly what he did, nudging the situation along until they were all able to cast aside doubts and inhibitions. He was just being more overt this time by playing into the whole movie-making scenario.

"What are you, the director?" Faye looked beyond him, at the phone, and her mind whirred. The set up turned her on immensely, and that astonished her. It was recording, right now. *Am I really doing this*?

Jai nodded. "What mood are we in?"

Garth rested a possessive hand on her hip. "Horny."

"Me too," Faye whispered. It was the truth, but as she said it a sense of mischief flitted through her. "I'm surrounded by all this high-powered testosterone, all this strength and virility, I can't help it. It makes me want to offer myself…"

Jai leaned over and cupped her chin, staring down into her eyes. "Offer yourself, huh?"

His eyes glinted. He looked dangerously aroused, and he was in charge.

Faye's pulse raced.

He drew her to her feet then changed places with her, dropping down onto her spot on the bed. "Why don't you offer yourself by stripping for us? We're waiting."

Her heart thundered in her chest. She was on the spot, and she could either take up the challenge or back out, and that would mean missing the opportunity to watch the way this would unfold, over and again, after the event. Heady with arousal, she stared down at them. Her two lovers. Both of them were aroused, there was no hiding that. She took a deep breath. The camera was behind her. Jai had put her there on purpose.

"Show us what you've got." Jai gestured at her clothing then stroked his hand over his fly, as if making her a promise.

Garth cocked his head on one side.

Faye stared at the headboard beyond them for a moment to level her head. A few days ago she'd slumbered in that bed, never for one moment thinking something like this would ever happen to her. It thrilled her that it had. *Don't chicken out now. You'll always regret it.*

Reaching for her hem, she shimmied her dress up and off, nice and slow, playing to the mood. When she undid her bra she turned away from them and faced the camera. Glancing down at it, she saw the red light shining at her. *Will I be watching this footage alone, next week, remembering? Will they want to see it, or is it only my souvenir?*

She didn't want to think about that—about it being over next week—so she dropped the bra and turned back with her hands covering her breasts.

Garth stared at her openly, riveted.

Jai looked on with heavy-lidded eyes.

It struck her oddly. She had that effect on them, she was making them want her, both of them. It felt crazy-good, and it made her nerves dissipate. Instead she became wanton. She swayed her hips, growing heady with sexual empowerment, the very real availability of two lovers on her bed making her fling her hair back and enjoy the moment.

Teasing her fingers apart over her breasts, she allowed her nipples to be bared. The skin had knotted and peaked, her body throbbing. When the men stared, she clasped her nipples between her fingers, teasing them out before she pinched them between her thumb and forefinger. It felt so good that she moaned aloud as she swayed her hips.

"Bloody hell, Faye," Garth whispered.

Jai lifted up on to one elbow. "Take your panties off and touch yourself. We want to see you doing that."

Slowly easing her thumbs under the band on her knickers, she eased them down over her hips and thighs, then dropped them to the floor a stepped out of them. Her over-the-knee black stockings were still on, as were her high heels, but she liked that and she figured they did too. She put her left hand on her hip and with the right she stroked her finger back and forth over her pussy.

Jai gave a deep approving moan, like someone savouring a fine wine.

Her lips twitched. It gave her such a rush, behaving like this, teasing them, doing as they suggested but knowing it would make them even more eager and ready for her. She widened her stance and eased two fingers into the damp groove of her pussy. Her clit thrummed as she made contact in a fleeting stroke. Inhaling sharply, she paused, then stroked again. Her body was so keyed up by the exhibitionism that she was almost ready to come on the spot.

Garth's lips parted and he looked desperate to see more.

Her clit burned when she massaged it between two fingers.

"I can't see properly," Jai said. "Put one foot upon the bed, open your legs to us."

Swaying, she forced herself to pause. Altering her position carefully, she did as instructed. A fever of embarrassment rushed over her when she realised how thoroughly the new position displayed her intimate places. It made her feel so exposed, but she followed his command nonetheless, because he made her want to do that—to be brazen and lusty and to show them everything. Those hungry eyes watching her fingers move over her slick folds drove her on, and she put both hands down, opening herself up.

"Oh yes, that's much better," Jai said approvingly, his mouth lifted at one corner.

Her pulse raced. She delved deeper and drew her juices up to swirl over her clit. Tension gathered there with each stroke. Her core throbbed in time, her skin a rush of hot and cold. "I'm going to come."

"Good, we want to see you come." Jai gave a decadent smile. He loved this game.

She tried to imagine what the footage would look like, with her naked and masturbating for them, the two men arranged on either side of the bed, an empty space down the middle for her. She cried out as she climaxed, her entire body swaying.

"Come on, get on the bed." Jai gestured to her.

Panting for breath, she scrambled up between them. Her orgasm had only piqued her interest, and the bulge in Jai's jeans reminded her he hadn't come, despite the pleasure he'd given her today. He'd also watched her and Garth at the building site, but he'd been waiting. She reached for his zipper, looking at him.

He nodded, encouraging her.

She fumbled with the button and pulled the zipper down, struggling to get the waistband on his shorts over the erect penis beneath. When his cock bowed out, long and hard and beautiful, it made her mouth water.

"You like that, do you." Jai gave her a querying look and wrapped his hand around the base of his cock pointing it toward her.

She ducked her head and ran her tongue over the crown, tasting him.

Garth interrupted. "Jesus, Jai, this is driving me crazy."

"No way. This time I'm first in line. Remember, I'm the director."

Faye had to lift her head to let out a chuckle. She kept her hand moving up and down his erection while she observed his body respond to her touch. The head grew darker still, the skin silky and taut as he lengthened in her hand, turning hard as iron. Her sex ached for it, but she also wanted to make him come with her mouth. It made her feel powerful, knowing she could give him pleasure that way.

While she continued her ministrations, Faye quickly found herself arranged by the two men. Jai had leaned against the pillows and moved onto his side, and when he encouraged her to lie down beside him she turned her face his way so she could continue her attentions to his beautiful cock. Garth manoeuvred her with his hands around her hips, positioning her so that her lower body was lying diagonally across the bed. Then he knelt at the side of the bed and opened her legs. With his hands on her inner thighs, he went down on her.

Faye pulled free and cried out when she felt him bury his face between her thighs, his mouth closing over her sensitive clit. Glancing at where the camera was recording from the dresser she realised what they had done and how this would look. Her body splayed across the bed, one man with his mouth on her pussy, while she took another man's cock into her mouth.

It felt wildly liberated and she revelled in it, her mouth sucking Jai off in time with the strokes of Garth's tongue up and down her folds and around her hard clit.

"Oh yes, that's really good," Jai said, with an effort. "And you must taste really good, because poor old Garth is in such a state he's having to jerk himself off."

That information sent Faye into overdrive and her climax loomed closer still. She glanced down and saw Garth's shoulder moving as he worked his erection, all the while loving her with his mouth. Then he grunted and his mouth moved over her sex folds faster still, as if he couldn't get enough and he devoured her, licking her juices while she melted all over again under his tongue. The intense three-way interaction put her into overdrive. Her core went into spasm, her clit pounding as she shuddered in release. It made her frantic, and she took Jai deep, stroking the head of his cock along the roof of her mouth, owning him completely when she felt him deep against her throat, and he swore in response.

Garth lifted his head. "Jesus, you taste so good."

He worked his cock hard then emitted a loud and prolonged moan of release.

Jai jerked, pulled back, and came. Faye refused to let him draw away completely, licking him and causing him to collapse back onto the bed. His dark eyes burned with pleasure, and he grasped her around the head, moving so that he could kiss her instead.

She was almost delirious with pleasure, outrageously sated by her brazen behaviour in front of the camera and richly pleasured by the two men that moved closer still, encapsulating her in a mutual embrace as the three of them revelled in the afterglow. Her hips undulated between them, her body still simmering on.

"Please," Garth begged, "take pity on me, you'll make me hard again."

Faye chuckled. When she glanced up at Jai his expression had grown thoughtful. A smile still lingered around his sensuous mouth, but he watched the two of them, overseeing them as they cuddled and wriggled and kissed.

He likes this, she realised. He liked the way they looked, cavorting on the bed together. Her mind filled with an image of them like a chain, with her the link between the two men, high as a kite because of the way they were interacting with her. For one blissful moment she let it fill her mind and blank out every other thought and feeling she'd ever had. It might only be for one wild weekend, but she wanted this memory to last forever.

Chapter Nine

"Sleep now," Garth said. "We'll leave you in peace."

Jai had pulled on his T-shirt and jockeys and got ready to go. "We'll make ourselves familiar with your DVD collection." He picked up her phone and switched it off. "Okay if I check the quality of the footage we got?"

Faye laughed. "Yeah, you check out the 'quality' why don't you."

Jai winked at her. "Don't worry. We'll keep the noise down."

Garth grabbed his clothes but hung back after Jai left. "What time do you want to go back to the house?"

Faye looked up at him in wonder.

He'd put his stack of clothes on the end of the bed and got busy tucking her in. He'd been serious when he said he'd do that. The last time she'd been tucked in to bed was when she was nine years old, but it felt good. She felt cherished.

He reached over and rested a kiss on her forehead. "How about I wake you around nine with a nice cup of tea."

Faye laughed softly. "Where have you been all my life?"

Garth didn't respond, but continued to stare down at her with a thoughtful expression. Eventually he gave a sheepish smile and kissed her forehead again, before following in Jai's footsteps, switching the light off as he went.

Faye sank back into her pillows and willed sleep to come. She had important work to do that night. It was now a matter of honour that she gained Garth a good outcome.

"You can't be serious." Garth perched on Faye's sofa and watched Jai in amazement.

Once they were in the sitting room, he'd quickly located an AV cable and connected it up to the TV. He was now kneeling at the side of Faye's television in just his shorts and socks, working at getting the phone linked up to the TV, and he looked entirely serious about the endeavour.

The TV screen flickered into life and it filled with the image of Faye's bottom as she began to strip. Garth immediately lost his train of thought.

Jai turned his way. "Come on, can you really resist?"

In view of what he was looking at, Garth found himself totally unable to answer the question, so he didn't say anything at all.

Jai took his silence as agreement, switched the TV to mute and joined Garth on the sofa. "Faye didn't mind me taking it to check it out. She's easy going, not like you."

Garth stared at the TV. "She's incredible."

"She certainly is. No regrets then?"

They both spoke without taking their eyes from the screen.

"No. Do you think she'd have gone to bed with me, just me, if you hadn't been there?"

Jai gave a wry laugh. "Hark at Mr Glum. We've got this incredible woman and the three of us are having a wild time, and still you want to brood about whether it's right or wrong."

Garth looked at Jai. "No, it does feel right. I just need to know if she's attracted to me or just…the whole package deal."

Jai glanced at him from the corner of his eye then kept watching the screen. "Sometimes you have to accept that the stars are in alignment and things happen for a reason beyond anything we might have planned in life."

"I know, but you've got more experience with these things than me. I just can't get my head around it. When it's happening it's all good and I can't get enough."

"So I noticed."

Garth felt surprisingly comfortable talking about it. "Don't look so surprised."

"I am surprised. I thought you might be a bit coy, you know…like you might struggle to get it up in front of me."

Garth shrugged. "Under ordinary circumstances maybe I would, and I'm not ashamed of that. Faye is not ordinary circumstances."

"No, she isn't." Jai laughed. "Man, you really go for it once you let rip."

"Do you have to comment on my performance? This is exactly why I can't believe I'm sharing a woman with you."

"We've shared pretty much everything else for the last ten years. We've studied and worked together. We've invested in each other through our joint business. We pulled together a wreck of a house, and we even made the decision to bring in an exorcist—I remember what a ball ache that one was with you."

"Faye is not an exorcist."

"No, but if I recall correctly that's what you thought we needed to begin with."

"How the hell would I know there are friendly ghost hunters? It's hardly my area of expertise."

"I didn't know that either, neither of us did until you saw Faye's ad. I'm just saying we made that decision together. We often do. We've even spent a Christmas together."

"That was only because my parents were away on a cruise."

"Yeah, and my family took pity on you."

Garth shot Jai a warning glance.

Jai shrugged. "Look buddy, it shouldn't be any different to all the other things we share. Yes, it's different because it's a relationship and we're all real people with real feelings, but why feel the need to analyse and question it? Some things in life are outside the realms of predictability, but they can still be embraced and enjoyed."

Somewhat reluctantly, Garth nodded. He knew Jai was right, but he couldn't shake the uneasy feeling that she might not have slept with him, if it had just been him at the house the night before.

"Faye is very attracted to you, there's no doubt about that."

"She's also attracted to you."

"That's how it usually works in a threesome."

"You're deliberately missing my point."

"Look, buddy, if I had to put money on it, I think she would have had a relationship with you. The fact that she had a fantasy about a threesome probably made things develop more quickly, that's all."

Garth stared at the screen, watching himself going down on Faye. He thought he might have been embarrassed seeing himself that way, but he couldn't take his eyes off Faye, watching the way she responded. "Thank you, for taking charge in there, it was out of my league."

"It's the natural order of things. I just happen to be a more sophisticated man than you."

Garth shook his head, but didn't respond.

"Look, it's no big deal. I care about you, buddy."

Garth figured this was probably Jai at his most serious. "I appreciate that. I care about you too."

Jai stretched his arms out along the back of the sofa, easing back into a more relaxed position. He nodded down at his groin. "In that case how about you give me a quick hand job. This home movie has given me a stonking hard on."

Garth jerked away along the sofa. "Get lost."

Jai laughed. "Your face! Absolutely priceless."

Chapter Ten

Back at the house that night Faye oscillated between the men while they ate pizza, sitting on Garth's lap in order to feed him a piece, then doing the same with Jai. The euphoria she was experiencing after twenty-four hours of fabulous double-barrelled sex and so much experimentation had made her high.

"I need to focus on your resident ghost," she murmured while she watched Jai devour his late night pizza.

His arm tightened on her waist.

"Don't you think you should tuck us in before you get started on your paranormal work?" Garth said. "It's only fair pay back, after all." He grinned.

She reached out and gave him a playful punch on the shoulder. "Like I can trust you to end it on a…tuck."

Jai chortled.

She gave in to their request and lay on the bed between them while they watched TV. She had to forbid any more hanky panky for the time being, lest it made her forget Maud.

When she got up to go, both men turned their heads to look at her.

"I'm going to go investigate. I have a feeling your ghost might be lurking around downstairs again."

"She doesn't come up and watch us does she?" Jai asked the question, eyeing her naked body as he did so.

"If I find her, maybe I'll ask." She gave him a quick smile and before he had a chance to quiz her any more she flung the shirt on and buttoned it as she left. Behind her she could hear them speaking, their voices lowered but still audible.

"Surely you don't intend to sleep in my bed now?" Garth said, apparently infuriated at the idea of it, even though he'd been happily about to doze off with all three of them in it moments before.

"Of course I am. What, we shared Faye, and now you won't share your bed?"

"It just feels weird, without Faye in the middle."

Faye paused and smiled to herself.

"Can I remind you that we shared a bed when we did that visit to Rotterdam, and you didn't complain then?" Jai's voice was filled with irony.

"That was different. The company secretary booked us a double room because they all thought we were…together."

"Yes, and that seems to be happening a lot recently," Jai pointed out, "you really are in danger of destroying my reputation as a ladies' man."

Garth muttered an inaudible response then Jai demanded a larger share of the quilt.

Their voices faded as Faye made her way across the apartment and down the stairs but she found herself much amused by their banter. Again it reminded her of an old married couple who knew each other well enough that they could have a whine every now and again and get away with it.

As she darted down the stairs, she went over her plans. She needed to actively engage with Maud so she intended to be pushier with her. On two previous occasions she'd been able to request the ghosts came to her, once she knew their names. She'd been a bit further down the line with them, but she would have to give it a try with Maud.

The hallway was dark, but the streetlight outside cast an eerie glow into the hallway. It made her feel cold. Cold was not good. Faye braced herself and headed in to the kitchen. They'd left that light on, thankfully, and she breathed a bit easier.

"Right, here goes," she whispered to herself, then closed her eyes and visualised the room as it might have been many years ago, when Maud was here. She stood in the centre of the kitchen, slowly turning around on the spot. "I'm here for you, Maud Radisson. I've come to visit with you, in your space."

Nothing happened at first. She cocked her head and listened, her senses on high alert. Outside a lone bird twittered and she caught the distant rumble of a night bus, but nothing indoors. The floor beneath her feet felt so cold and she wished she'd stopped to put some socks on. She looked into each corner of the room. This was the place to which Maud gravitated. Why? The newspaper article noted that she had been transporting catering supplies when she'd skidded on ice.

"Are you here? Will you talk to me again?"

At the window the sky was lightening. She went to fill the kettle.

Her fingertips began to tingle, and very soon her entire body tingled too, her awareness altering. A paranormal presence was close by, the atmosphere filling with static energy, that unique aura given off by a spirit trapped in time.

Faye urged herself to act normally, to be sociable, hoping that would make Maud linger a while. She wanted Maud to be more comfortable this time. The woman must have been lonely. She needed a friend. There was jealousy in her but no overt aggression, no throwing things or shattering glass. She'd come across that before and it wasn't a pleasant barrier to surmount. A little jealousy she could deal with.

By the time the kettle was on the boil Faye had located the mugs. She spooned coffee into the mug. Then she felt Maud's presence materialising behind her. Faye tried not to react too overtly. Once the kettle clicked off, she glanced back over her shoulder.

Maud stood in the doorway, observing her with curiosity.

Faye smiled. "I'm sorry, did I disturb you when I spoke your name?"

"My fault for giving it to you, I s'pose." Maud shrugged. "Not like I've got anything else to do." She strode into the kitchen, lifting her chin as she did so. "Why are you here? Did they hire you for the weekend?"

Ah, she was back in good form, and she had questions of her own. That boded well. "Yes, they did hire me," Faye responded. Then it dawned on her that Maud meant something entirely different to hunting ghosts. "Oh, I see. You mean for sex?"

"That is what you've been doing with them." The comment was definitely tinged with jealousy and the ghost eyed Faye warily. She sat up on one of the work surfaces, perching on the edge, her feet resting on a chair below.

Faye had the feeling she often took up that position, perhaps observing Jai and Garth while they were in here. "That wasn't why I came here. Actually, the new owners hired me because they wanted me to find out more about you."

"Did they?" Maud's expression altered, as if she hadn't considered that option. A faint smile passed over her face.

"Yes, they sometimes sense your presence, so they got curious. They contacted me because I can help."

Maud rested her elbows on her knees and her chin on her hands. Faye felt more hopeful. This could only work in her favour.

Then Maud's gaze returned to her and her smile disappeared. "But you had sex with them, both of them."

"Yes, that just sort of happened." Slight fib there, because it didn't just happen. Both she and Jai had been edging it forward from the moment the subject of threesomes had been mentioned.

"Well, I can't says that I wouldn't do the same," Maud responded, somewhat sarcastically. "They're both attractive blokes and if they like three in the bed, all the better for you, or so I would imagine."

"Not something you've tried yourself?"

"No, a couple of the girls here had clients who were into that. I've never done it with two men at once." She stared off into the distance, then blinked into the light at the window. "You asked if I died here. Well, I didn't."

"How did you die?" She asked the question tentatively. Did Maud even know? Was it a missing memory, something she chose not to accept because of the circumstances surrounding the event?

Maud gave a sad laugh, and it seemed to echo around kitchen endlessly. "If you'd asked my pals, the girls who worked here, they'd have said I died of a broken heart." She rose to her feet then turned away, but paused. "It's not what you think though," she added, defensively.

Frustrated, Faye observed her spirit began to fade. *Not what I think*? She didn't know quite what to think. Maud was being cryptic, although it was obvious that she did have some sort of a grief that she carried still.

"Please don't go," she called out.

Maud's physical presence hovered indistinctly.

Instinctively, she said the first thing that came to mind. "What will I tell Garth and Jai? They want to know all about you."

The spirit form solidified. "They seem to be more interested in you now."

"Just because there is an attraction between us, doesn't mean they've forgotten you. They want to know more. They wouldn't have hired me otherwise. The sex thing, well, it's not the real reason I came here, is it?"

Mercifully Maud lingered. She sighed and wandered to the sink, glancing out of the window. "Look, I don't blame you. Just ignore me, I'm jealous."

Faye experienced an odd visual loop and saw Maud repeat that action of looking out the window over and over, through time. Maud seemed constantly drawn to the window. Faye stepped closer to her side and observed her expression.

Her eyes were focused on the yard outside. Her mouth was still downturned at the corners, but when Faye made a sound Maud turned her way and gave a reluctant smile.

"You have a beautiful smile," Faye told her.

Maud, who had presumably been alone without flattery for several decades, smiled again. Faye felt her opening up, and moved on rapidly. "The guys, Jai and Garth, they are very interested in your connection to this house." A different tactic. "What was it like when you used to live here?"

"It was a brothel, fancy place mind you."

"In the 1960s?"

"Yes," Maud replied, and again she perched on the edge of the cabinet and rested her high-heeled peep toe court shoes on the seat of the chair. This time she seemed more settled. She put her chin on her hands. "It was an exciting time, the music and the people. We had a lot of top bods here, overseas politicians, people with money, great parties." She winked then, and Faye felt warmth rekindling in Maud's spirit.

"Government people used to come here for long lunch breaks." She looked round the place as if remembering, and as she did Faye received a rush of information from her—images and colours, smells and noise. "Although mostly they weren't eating lunch, if you see what I mean."

Faye began to see the place as Maud did in her memories.

The rooms were smaller, the building more divided with heavy curtains at the windows and expensive flocked wallpaper. It was packed with people, men in suits and women in all sorts of getups, from cocktail dresses to kinky underwear, while one woman carried a drinks tray wearing a tight black and white uniform with a bow tie and an apron. It took a moment for Faye to realise she was looking at Maud as she had been, serving cocktails. The woman in the vision stopped and smiled as a man leant forward from his seat and put his hand under her apron, fondling her thigh.

When Maud spoke again, Faye jolted back to the present moment.

"Mad times we had." Maud nodded out in the hallway. "That front room where the big desk is now, it used to be one of the parlours. Comfy it was too. All plush velvet and deep seats, lots of cushions."

She looked back at Faye for the first time in several minutes. "That's the only thing I don't like about these two," she added conspiratorially, her cockney accent more apparent than ever. "What they've done to this place…it's so…sparse." She shook her head as if disappointed in the men.

"It's the fashion now, they call it minimalism."

"Needs a woman's touch it does." As she said it she gave Faye a sidelong glance, as if she still wondered about her role.

"So you were one of the party girls who worked here?" Faye asked the question in an attempt to move her back onto more fruitful grounds.

She reeled from how close to Maud's memories she'd got. Vivid and real, it was like nothing she'd ever experienced before. In her past interactions with the spirit world she'd been a listener not a virtual participant. What did it mean? Were her skills reaching a new level, or was it just Maud and the nature of their two worlds, cross-crossing on an edge of kinky eroticism?

"No, not exactly one of the girls. I was hired as a cook. That was a joke. Mostly I had to keep up an endless supply of canapés and cocktails."

"Ah, I see. That's why you favour the kitchen."

"I spent a lot of time in here, and we had a lot of laughs I here too, when the girls were on a break. Although I was called on to do all sorts."

"Serving?"

Maud nodded. "That, and wilder stuff. Sometimes I was called on to strut around in my uniform with a whip, while one of the girls did her stuff with a bloke. Apparently he got really turned on by being watched while he was at it." She rolled her eyes. "The things I saw!"

"I bet." Faye wondered if she had observed her with Jai and Garth.

"If they needed me they used to stand on the staircase and shout out for the watcher, and that meant me."

"Have you watched the new owners with a woman?"

"You mean when you are with them?"

Faye nodded. Had Garth brought anybody else up to the top floor apartment?

"No, you're the only guest who's made it past the ground floor." She jerked her head upwards. "And I don't go up there."

Why not? If she liked to watch, that would be the best place to be.

"Don't you like what they've done to the rooms up there?" She asked the question tentatively, because she immediately felt as she had pushed into a sensitive area. What could it be? It wasn't the site of her death. They'd already established that had happened outside the house.

"I had to live up there for a while, that's all. It was a bad time for me."

"And when you go up there the memories come?" She knew she was walking the line now, but she had to tease the information out to put the pieces together.

"The memories are always with me," she said bitterly. "The pain comes if I'm up there alone, thinking on it, like I was." Maud stared off into space for a while and her image faded then became clear again.

"Tell you what, if you feel sorry for me, you should have it off with them two down here, where I can watch."

"You really are a naughty girl, aren't you?"

"I wasn't always, believe me. Good Catholic upbringing I had, and a strict mam. She hated that I was working here, even though I was only doing the catering. I got paid a lot better than being a dinner lady in a school but she didn't care. It was all about what the neighbours would think, with 'er.

"Do you know what, when I first came to work here I didn't even realise the stuff people got up to. I thought married couples went to bed to make babies." She gave a self-deprecating laugh. "I soon learnt there was much more to it than that."

"That must have been a baptism by fire, learning about sexuality the way you did."

"It came as a shock at first, but the girls were always talking about what they got up to with clients, in here." She nodded around the kitchen. "While they were on a break. I soon got used to it."

"It must have been very…arousing, hearing about it all, and seeing it, too." Faye was getting aroused on the transferred memories. Although Maud hadn't been one of the working girls here, she was clearly no blushing debutante and relished a little sex gossip, not to mention her voyeuristic streak.

"It was." Her eyes narrowed. "And I've been thinking about the sexy times a lot, since those two arrived here." She observed Faye a moment longer then leant toward her, whispering. "Tell me, which one of them two is the best lover?"

Her head went from side to side as she asked the naughty question, her shoulders lifting. At first she'd been so still, and watchful. It was as if her deeply buried mannerisms were rising to the surface now that she interacted with someone. Faye was delighted. It meant she was getting somewhere, and it was a bonus to witness Maud opening up.

"Tell you what, I'll cut you deal," Faye said, matching up to Maud's emergent cocky attitude with some of her own.

"You tell me about the favourite lover you had, and I'll tell you about those two."

"What, I get your two for the price of my one?" Maud grinned.

"That's the deal, take it or leave it." Faye leaned against the fridge with one shoulder. This was how it was with the women who had worked here, she was sure of it.

"We understand each other, I like that." Maud braced her hands on her knees and nodded. "We had a girl here like you, liked two at the same time. Sandra her name was." Maud stared over at her, as if comparing her to Sandra. "She'd have loved them two."

"What woman in their right mind wouldn't like them two?" Faye commented, wondering about Sandra, and grateful for her too. Maud was relaxing, and she had revealed things about herself.

Maud nodded enthusiastically.

Presumably a woman couldn't have worked somewhere like this if she was embarrassed by the subject, even if she was only responsible for the catering. Maud seemed to like chatting with someone understood that. It wasn't called the swinging Sixties for nothing, Faye reflected. In her quick foray into the newspapers from that time she'd discovered that there were several scandals around high-class call girls and high profile government ministers. Had this house been one of the infamous brothels that had brought down several ministers living the high life before their cover was blown apart? "Tell me about your favourite."

"Ah, well now, my favourite." Again Maud's expression grew reminiscent. "The best lover I ever had wasn't one of the customers. He was the delivery man. He came here every week…you know, with the champagne and the stuff for the canapés. From Fortnum and Mason, he was. Top class nosh for the nobs." She laughed softly. "This one time the boss lady hadn't left me enough money to pay him, and I only had a bit of my own money which I needed for my electricity meter back at my bedsit. So he told me that he would cover the short fall, just this once, if I went with him in the back of his van."

"What was he like?"

"Paulo was Italian. A tall man he was, good-looking. He didn't say a lot, but he knew what he liked. I remember him giving me a hand up into the van. It felt outrageous to be doing it in there, to write-off the bill, but you see I'd fancied him for ages so I was quite happy with the suggestion."

She wrapped her arms around herself and leant forward, smiling. "The van was full of the most delicious smells, spiced meats, fancy pastries and exotic fruit, all this posh grub." She inhaled, and Faye saw that aspect of her character in full glory then.

"He didn't mess around. He liked to kiss, but once that was done he didn't even wait to take our clothes off, he just told me to bend over a stack of boxes and did me from behind. It felt so naughty, and he had this thing he did." Her eyes rounded.

Faye's attention was already well and truly hooked, but she really wanted to know what Paulo's thing was.

"When he got a good rhythm going he spanked my bottom. Glory be," she exclaimed, "it was the strangest thing in the world, but it made it even better!"

Her mirth and her sexy tale were contagious, and Faye laughed.

"So, your turn now. Tell me about them two." Maud nodded her head upstairs. She was almost challenging in her intensity. Maud clearly liked to be engaged, and she'd been lacking that.

"I think I must be a little like your naughty friend Sandra, I'm enjoying them both."

"I'm enjoying them too. It's the most fun I've had in ages, seeing them two here."

"Apart from the builders?"

Maud gave her an appreciative nod. "Yes, those chaps were quite the entertainers. Apart from the occasional reference to football and ale and food, all they seemed to do was compare notes on their sex lives. Their wives and girlfriends must have had their ears on fire."

Faye wondered if she imagined it, or whether Maud's eyes were really twinkling in her ghostly face as she related her thoughts on the builders. "I'm sure the builders would have loved having a glamorous woman like you watch them as they went about their work."

The bond between them was growing, for which Faye was grateful.

"There was this one chap, he was like some sort of an assistant, did most of the carting around of bags of plaster and the like, and he seemed to sense I was here. Of course he didn't understand it and he couldn't actually see me, but he always looked over his shoulder when I came into the room. I know it'll probably sound daft to you," she added and paused, "but it gave me a little boost, you know, thinking that he was looking at me."

It seemed to Faye that what Maud missed most of all was being appreciated as a feminine woman, which even in her ghostly form she was. The height of sixties allure, she wore long false eyelashes, her big smoky eyes the focal point in a pretty oval face. It was the classic Jean Shrimpton look, hair stacked high and corkscrew tendrils. Quintessential Sixties style with the fitted mini dress and big shoes.

Faye was so busy admiring her that she didn't become aware of another person approaching until Maud looked toward the doorway and fell silent on her reminiscing.

"No-show from our ghost then?"

The male voice made Faye jump. She'd been far away, enjoying the exchange of gossip and transported back to the 'sixties by Maud's storytelling.

Garth stood in the doorway. He had put on a black dressing gown that made him look rather like a spy from a glamorous movie. And he looked at her with a brooding, almost predatory expression, as if he wanted her back in his arms.

Faye exchanged glances with Maud. It was then that Faye realised she'd paused in the conversation just as he'd arrived, and he hadn't realised she was conversing with Maud.

When she didn't respond, he looked a bit awkward. "I'm not interrupting your alone time, am I?"

Maud shook her head vigorously.

"Not at all," Faye said quickly. "I was just wondering about what the house was like back in the 'sixties."

Garth walked toward her. "It was a maze of different sized rooms, when we came in. Looked as if there had been lots of sublets."

Maud covered her mouth with her fingers, but she was grinning.

Faye looked at Garth from under her lashes, infected by Maud's mood. "I guess they needed lots of rooms for all the sexy action going on here."

"I can't get over that, about it being a fancy bordello. It's hard to imagine." He glanced around his kitchen, but didn't seem to sense Maud's presence at all.

Faye observed that point and wondered if it was because Maud was hanging back, watching. Perhaps it was only when she made an effort toward the men that they became aware of her. It was something she'd have to make notes on, she realised. Whatever the reason for his lack of awareness, it tickled Faye. Garth had desire in his eyes. The invisible presence of Maud—who seemed to be thoroughly enjoying Garth in his dressing gown and exchanged glances with Faye every now and then—made the sexual tension of the moment heighten for Faye.

Maud had a wayward, naughty look about her. Faye responded to it, riding on the wave of the moment. "What, even when the three of us are going at it in your bed, you can't imagine the sexy action that went on in bygone times here?"

Garth huffed a laugh. The humour in his eyes turned to molten heat, his thoughts obviously wandering. "You've got a point."

Faye winked at Maud, who seemed to egg her on.

She turned her attention to the refrigerator, opening the door as if having a rifle through the contents. The masculine shirt she had borrowed covered her up quite well, but when she bent over to look into the fridge it rode up, exposing the tops of her thighs, and probably more. "I was wondering what you have in here."

Garth joined her beside the fridge.

As soon as he did, she shut it and focused on him. It was a risk with Maud, who had initially been jealous, but Maud gave her so much encouragement she had to go with it. Stepping closer to him, Faye stroked her hands down over the silky black fabric covering his chest. "I say, this is a rather sexy number. It suits you."

Garth looked at her as if he wasn't sure she was being serious. "Really? It was a gift from my mother."

"Your mother has good taste, and she wanted you to look good." Faye looked at Maud. "I'm sure anyone would agree with me."

Encouraged, Maud slipped from her perch on the table and sidled closer to them. Faye knew what this was about. She'd promised she'd share what it was like with them, what better way than a demonstration? She touched him through the sexy garment, feeling the virile strength of the man beneath.

Garth gave a slow, sexy grin. He covered her hands with his. "If you keep doing that, this erection you got started will demand real action." He took the opportunity to push the shirt she was wearing down her shoulders and off.

Faye shivered and moved closer. She noticed that he was more straightforward when Jai wasn't there. She lowered one of her hands and wrapped it around his hardening cock, moving the silky fabric of his gown over it as she did so.

Garth groaned. His he rested his head back against the wall and he spread his feet, widening his stance. His lips were pressed together tightly, and he lowered his eyelids as he watched what she was doing.

Faye had already been turned on by Maud's stories about the girls and the delivery man, and now Garth was here. Garth, the man who'd engaged her with his voice over the phone. The one who had made her feel cherished and special even while he was banging her to oblivion. "What, you mean like this?"

"You're a minx," he commented.

"You better believe it."

When he shut his eyes for a moment, she nodded at Maud.

Maud moved closer still, observing as Faye gradually allowed the fabric to slip away and Garth's erection bowed out from his hips.

Wrapping her free hand around the column of his neck, she smiled up at him. Her pussy tingled with arousal. The presence of a very erect, very willing cock had that effect on a girl, especially one belonging to such an adorable man.

She purred her approval as she looked at his cock.

"You're going to make me come," he muttered beneath his breath.

Faye stood on tiptoe and kissed his mouth. "You bet I am," she said as she pulled away. "Preferably over the table with you fucking me from behind."

Garth shook his head in disbelief.

The head of his cock felt slippery and she couldn't think of anything she wanted more than to be bent over the table and for him to run her through with this glorious erection. Maud would enjoy it too, she thought, feeling wildly naughty. It flashed through her mind that this bonded her with Maud, which was what she came to do. How ironic, and yet how perfect.

"I'd like that," Garth responded, his voice harsh with restraint.

"Can I join the party?" It was Jai, and he stood in the doorway to the kitchen.

Maud immediately gravitated to him, pacing across his path and causing him to draw to a halt. He looked confused for a moment but shook it off.

"Of course you can," Faye responded. "Then we've got everyone present and accounted for." She wondered if he would catch the drift.

Garth shot a look at Jai, but he continued to remain hard in her hand and his cock reached.

Looking into his eyes Faye could see that he liked the fact Jai watched her hand moving up and down on his erection, and he also liked the fact her attention was only on him right at that moment. Was there a challenge there in his eyes too? If she had to guess, she would say that challenge was to force Jai to watch while he had her all to himself, like that time at the building site.

Remembering how driven he'd been, how insatiable, her arousal soared. She felt dizzy. Like her, Garth had discovered his exhibitionist streak and it empowered him wildly during sex. He didn't know the half of it, she thought to herself. Maud looked entranced and kept nodding at Faye, encouraging the show.

"She's here, isn't she?" Jai declared.

For the first time, Faye thought he looked a bit disturbed by the set up. Jai, who was so chilled and esoteric and so together. "Maybe."

"Seriously?" Garth glanced around the room. "You really are a minx."

"So is Maud, believe me." Faye was glad Garth wasn't too bothered.

"Hmm, it suddenly feels as if there are four people in this relationship." Jai gave a confused gesture—lifting his shoulders and opening his hands to the heavens. He seemed much more sensitive to her presence than Garth.

"What...four participants bothers you when three doesn't?"

"Yeah, I'm really freaked out."

Was it genuine? Faye had a hard time determining where the joking ended and the honesty began. Perhaps that was their way of being honest with each other. "Come on, guys, you know she's always around. That's why I'm here in the first place, right?"

Jai broke into a grin. "You believed me, I love it."

Faye suddenly knew why Garth lost his rag with his friend. She picked up her abandoned shirt, bunched it in her hands hand threw it at him. "Shut up. I hate you!"

When she looked at Garth, he laughed and grabbed her into his arms.

"Come on, you don't hate him. He's a prat, I know. But you don't hate him." He looked over at his buddy, and she thought she saw fondness in his eyes. "He's entertaining, in his own way."

Part of her wanted to stomp off and leave them to their buddy-buddy thing, part of her wanted to dive into it and enjoy. She tugged out of Garth's grip and turned her back on him. Shimmying up and down against him, she carried on. "Maud told me what she thinks of this kinky relationship of ours."

If she'd wanted to harness the erotic tension of the moment, she surely did. Garth snatched her against him, holding her still. Jai stared at her. From beyond she saw Maud was there, watching.

"What does she think?" Jai scoured the room again, as if looking for her.

"She thought you bought me, to share."

"Why would she think that?" Garth asked.

She turned her head to look up at him.

Garth wore a curious expression.

"Because she worked here, and it was a whore house."

"Oh. Right." Garth looked embarrassed by the misunderstanding, which made Faye want to hug him, but she couldn't.

"Was Maud a prostitute?" he asked.

Maud rose to her feet. The conversation had her attention in a different way, a specific way. Faye's heart beat wildly. For the first time, she really had Maud's attention. She knew why. Maud wanted to be remembered by someone, in a positive light. Well, that wasn't any revelation, and Faye chastised herself for not realising it before. It was a basic human need.

"No, she was the caterer. She worked here in the kitchens, that's why she lingers here in particular. This room was special to her, and it went beyond her role as a cook and caterer. I want her to tell me why." She stared across at Maud. "But she hasn't. Not yet."

"Is she watching us now?" Garth's erection was solid at her back.

Faye span around in his arms. "Yes, and she wants a show, she wants to see you in action."

He kissed her hungrily, his tongue exploring her lips, her mouth. Faye wrapped her hand around his cock, loving the way it felt, and knowing their two observers would see.

Garth broke the kiss suddenly and he was wild-eyed. He turned her round, bending her over the kitchen table as she had suggested.

Faye gasped as she felt the cool wood against her bared breasts. Garth pressed his hand to the small of her back, so that she was flat to the surface.

It felt good, damn good, and Faye whimpered, entirely locked to his will. Something had empowered him, and she liked how it felt with him being in charge and masterful.

His hands roamed over her exposed bottom, kneading the flesh, his thumbs opening up her crease. It was outrageously deliberate and her sense of self-awareness multiplied. All the attention was on her, and she was bent over, exposed, vulnerable, and desperate as a cat in a heat.

Turning her face she looked at Jai. He was stroking his cock. Maud stood right beside him, watching. From time to time she glanced over at the table, then back to Jai.

Pangs of need shot through Faye as Garth kneaded her flesh, easing her buttocks apart, his cock nudging into her sex. Watching Jai and Maud made it all the more steamy.

Then Garth grunted with primitive pleasure when her sex sucked him in. Sliding deep, he filled her to the hilt.

"Oh yes." She reached for the far edge of the table, gripping on to it to gain purchase.

"You okay, precious?" When she moaned agreement and nodded her head frantically, he thrust again. "Jesus, Faye. You're so hot and wet."

The set-up drove her crazy. She was already close to coming.

He thrust hard.

Awash with sensation, she cried out.

"Too much?"

"No!" She bit her lip when she saw Jai chuckle.

She thrust her hips back, pleasure spilling from her core. He filled her completely. She came fast and hot, her core in spasm.

"Oh yes, I feel you," Garth panted, stroking her back as her whole body shuddered in release. "Can you take some more?"

He began to move again, shallow strokes at first. The action seemed to make her climax spin out even longer.

"Yes, give it to me, hard." Mumbling her encouragement she gave herself over to his will, her body quickly building toward another orgasm as he rode her.

Jai had his cock out of his shorts and was wanking vigorously, his other hand cupping his balls.

It was such an arousing sight that Faye moaned and thrashed, wishing she could have both of them inside her at once.

Her inner thighs were slick with juices and her breasts were crushed to the wooden surface, rubbing and stinging wildly—and yet it felt so good, like she'd never been more alive.

Garth swore and held tight to her buttocks anchoring her on his cock. He was so deep. Wedged against her most sensitive spot, she felt his cock lurch. She wriggled and flexed, on the verge of coming again. He squeezed her buttocks together. Acute sensation roared through her, multiple orgasms.

As she tried to gather her faculties, she heard a woman's voice.

"That was the best fun ever."

She lifted her head.

Maud waved her fingertips at her, then flitted away.

Chapter Eleven

"I think this is the most lazy, self-indulgent Sunday I have ever spent." Faye sighed contentedly and rested her head on Garth's shoulder.

After the shenanigans during the night before, they'd spent all day in bed, chatting and watching movies. Jai had volunteered to go shopping for supplies, and Garth had been holding her in his arms as if he was afraid she would get up and leave too.

"I think I've bonded with Maud now, it should be easier to chat next time I see her."

"Bonded, is that what you call it?"

"You know how girls are, always gossiping about fellas and sex."

"You really do think of ghosts as friends."

"They aren't all that way, but Maud and I found some common ground, that's for sure." Laughter bubbled up inside her.

"Don't rush to chase her off." His tone grew serious and he kissed her on the end of her nose.

Faye's laughter faded. Why was it that simple little act made her feel all emotional? "I'll have to leave in the morning anyway. I work Monday through Wednesday in another job."

"I know, you mentioned that on the phone."

"I also mentioned that I hoped I could have this resolved by the end of the weekend." That was the plan.

"We've distracted you from the job, that's not an issue."

It still bothered Faye though.

"Can you come back tomorrow evening? You could stay over again. Go to work from here." He nuzzled her, kissing her ear lobe.

Faye gave a sigh of contentment. "I guess I could stay on the case that way, if you like."

"I like. Jai will too, I'm sure."

A moment later Jai appeared around the glass cube wall with two carrier bags in each hand. "You two haven't moved since I went out."

"You sure about that," Garth replied, and put a possessive hand on Faye's naked rump.

"Not entirely, no."

Faye got out of the bed. "I'll help with the unpacking."

She was just getting dressed when her phone rang. Rifling in her bag, she flicked it open.

"Faye, its Holly."

"Hi, Holly." While she spoke she snatched up an item of clothing to hold to her chest.

Garth had donned his black dressing gown and had taken two of the bags off Jai. Together they were discussing the contents as they headed to the kitchenette. Faye trailed after them, watching.

"Oh, I can tell you're busy." Holly's tone seemed tentative. She was no doubt getting vibes about Faye's current set up.

"Maybe."

"I believe I can hear a man's voice in the background. Is this business or pleasure I'm witnessing here?"

Faye chuckled. "Oh, let's call it a little of both." Plus some. She glanced over at the two men.

"I won't keep you long, I just called to tell you that Monica's on her way back to London."

"Really?" Faye's breath caught. She'd missed her big sister and she'd been worried about her too.

"Yup. They are due to land back at Heathrow early tomorrow morning and she's having a bit of a do at Cumbernauld's tomorrow evening. Kicks off about seven thirty."

"Wonderful, I'll be there." The thought of seeing her older sister made Faye's current state of happiness even greater.

"Will you be bringing anyone?"

"Maybe. I'll keep you posted." When she said her goodbyes, Faye glanced at her watch. So much was going on all at once but she had to focus on Maud too, because Faye felt she was nearly there with her..

When Maud appeared that night, Faye was sitting in the downstairs kitchen waiting expectantly.

Maud peered around. "What, not putting a show on for me tonight?"

"Nope. I want to chat."

Maud looked wary. "About what?"

"About you."

"Why?"

"Because you fascinate me. The things you said about the life you led. It's been amazing for me to talk with you, to experience your life, which is so unique and different to mine."

Maud looked mistrustful, maybe even irritated. She really had hoped to see the men. Faye could understand that.

"I told you the best bit, about the girls here and the parties."

"But there's more, isn't there?"

"Even if there is, why should I tell you?"

"Because talking about it might help, like therapy."

"Therapy?" Her expression was still suspicious.

Faye supposed there wasn't much therapy about in the Sixties. "It just means talking things out with someone who is sympathetic, someone who can perhaps help you to understand what happened."

Maud didn't look convinced, but she fell silent for a moment and looked at the window again. She was looking at the yard, Faye realised. The yard—the yard where the Fortnum and Mason delivery man came by.

"Was it Paulo who broke your heart?"

Maud shook her head, but she didn't look away from the window. "That was lust. We could have made more of it, maybe, but we didn't have the chance."

Faye was even more mystified. It wasn't Paulo. So why did the girls say Maud had had a broken heart? Then it came back to her. "It's not what you think," Maud had said, in one of their first discussions.

"He came this one day," Maud continued, "and I wasn't expecting him. Didn't have a delivery. He said he would be going back to Italy. He'd got a job back at home, freight driver, long haul. He asked me to go with him." She met Faye's stare. "I was tempted but it was too soon. I didn't know him well enough. It seemed like it would be a really risky thing to do, going to a country where I didn't know the language, with a man I barely knew."

"Was it sad to say goodbye?"

"In a way, yes. Paulo was all mine. He introduced me to wild things that were all mine and his, not second hand stories heard here in the kitchen."

That struck Faye oddly, because it mirrored her own experience with Jai and Garth. She'd been exposed to ménage relationships through her sisters, much as Maud was exposed to kinky sex through the working girls here. But meeting their own men was something else altogether.

"When I said no, he opened up an expensive bottle of champagne purloined from the back of his van." A smile passed over her expression as she remembered. "We drank it straight from the bottle as we toasted our futures."

"Then what happened?"

Maud's expression turned serious and her eyelids lowered. She meshed her hands together, then drew them to her face and covered her eyes.

Faye stiffened. She felt as if she'd been jolted through with an electric current, because an intense burst of silent emotion had come from Maud without warning. "Maud?"

"That's when I found out I was pregnant, after he'd gone."

Faye's throat felt constricted, so overwhelming was the emotion she felt from Maud. She'd made no mention of a baby before now, and Faye felt desperate, her empathy taking her right to the heart of the matter. She struggled to keep her voice level, to continue to draw Maud out, no matter how hard. "That must have been very difficult."

Maud hung her head. "The girls here told me to get rid of it. I couldn't do that, and I couldn't go home. My mam finished with me when she found out I'd got pregnant while I was working here."

Faye's mind raced through the possibilities. The car accident had been very close to the house. Had she left the place to have the child? No, the obituary surely would have mentioned that. "What did you do?"

"The girls here, they stood by me. I decided to have the baby and arrange for him to be adopted. I went to the nuns. They had this place over at Holborn. Big old Manor house it was. When I was six months gone I booked an appointment to ask for help. They agreed. I signed a form and then they showed me the place."

Her visual memories flitted through Faye's mind and she saw a sterile, cold place with a sombre mood.

"It had two staircases. One was for the girls giving birth to go upstairs to the maternity rooms, and the other was a big posh one where they made a show of carrying babies down to the people who were adopting."

It sounded archaic.

"I wanted it, but I dreaded going there."

"Was that when you lived upstairs on the top floor, when you were pregnant?"

"No, that came later."

Would she say more about it? "Did you give birth there, at the place in Holborn?"

Maud nodded. "When I went into labour one of the girls took me." Her lower lip trembled. "They took the baby from me straight away. He was big and healthy, a lovely boy. I scarcely got a look at him though, and they were taking him down the posh stairs to where his new mam and dad were waiting."

The immense sense of loss hit Faye hard, and she knew she only experienced a part of it, second-hand. She had no doubt that this was at the heart of Maud's lingering spirit, this secret child.

"You regretted it?"

"It was the right thing to do for the lad, but I lost my mind for a while there afterwards. That's when I stayed upstairs for a while. The girls wanted to keep an eye on me, told me I was suffering from grief." She fell silent again, staring off into the distance. "What broke my heart was that I didn't know if he had a better life. I wanted that for him, and the nuns said I could go back and they would tell me how he was. I never had the chance."

Because she died in her accident. Faye saw it all, the pieces of the puzzle finally slipping into place. "Would it help if you knew what had happened to him?"

"I'll never know."

"I may be able to help you. There are ways to find out."

Maud stared at her. "You would do that for me?"

The faint glimmer of hope she saw in Maud's eyes made her throat tighten and her eyes smarted with unshed tears. It was difficult to speak, but she wanted to. "I wish I could hold your hand and reassure you. I promise I will find out as much as I can for you."

Chapter Twelve

Faye slumped against the banisters in the hallway for a moment before going upstairs. The grief Maud had shared with her had been debilitating. But now she knew. The need to know about her baby boy was the stumbling block, the thing that stopped her spirit from resting in peace.

It took a few minutes to pull herself together, then Faye glanced at her watch and noticed it was only three hours until she had to be at work in the shop—her regular job, the one that paid the rent. Now she had the bit between her teeth with Maud, she wanted to press on. During her lunch break she could attempt to contact the adoption agency for guidance on where to begin the hunt for Maud's baby. It was a plan, and as she trudged upstairs, she grew hopeful about resolving Maud's concerns.

When she was on the second flight of stairs the sound of raised voices reached her. Garth and Jai were obviously awake, and they seemed to be having an argument.

She paused. She'd been hoping to get up there and wash her face and slip into bed while they slept. No such luck, and she didn't want them to see her in such an emotional mess. After her recent experience with Maud she was in no fit state to referee some disagreement they were having.

But then bits of the conversation reached her, and she heard her own name—and more—and she was drawn on, inexorably, listening all the while.

Garth stood in his kitchenette making coffee. He wanted to go to see how Faye was getting on, but after the previous incident he decided to keep well out of it. Yawning, he retied his dressing gown and went to the fridge for milk.

Jai entered the room.

"Coffee?"

"Mm. Please." Jai leaned up against the work surface and folded his arms across as his bare chest. "I was just thinking, maybe I should utilise that space downstairs after all, put a bit of furniture in there and move some of my stuff in."

"Touched a nerve did we?" It was about time Jai got his own place, and that would be one step nearer. He poured milk into two mugs of coffee.

"No, I just thought it would be more practical…if we are going to keep seeing Faye."

Garth stared at him. Jai had that knowing, amused look on his face, and—given the subject matter—it irritated Garth immensely. He shoved one of the mugs in Jai's direction. "So that's it, you've decided the outcome for everyone…you've decided that 'we are' going to keep seeing Faye."

Jai nodded then picked up his coffee and took a slug.

"This isn't some joke, some bit of fun. You've got to realise that I care about that woman."

"So do I."

Jai chose that moment to wander off into the sitting-room.

Garth stomped after him, infuriated. He'd assumed Jai would get bored and leave him and Faye to it. "What gives you the right to decide who sees who?"

Jai was perfectly calm. "With a woman like Faye, I figure she needs to know where she stands. If we want to take this seriously, we need to say so."

"I know that, but I don't need you to speak for me."

Jai put his coffee down. "That wasn't what you said on Saturday, when you thanked me for taking charge."

"That was different. I did not have experience in that situation. I'm fully able to state my intentions without you sticking your oar in."

"I get the feeling you weren't intending to share your intentions with me." Jai looked annoyed now too.

"Why should I? I thought you would get bored and bugger off."

Jai gave a heavily sarcastic response. "Gee, thanks buddy."

Garth's annoyance grew. It felt as if this was getting out of his control, and it meant too much for that to happen. "You know what I mean. You don't do the dating, commitment thing."

Jai gesticulated, as if he despaired. "Maybe I haven't before now, that doesn't mean I won't ever, not if I like a woman as much as I like Faye. Besides, what makes you think she would be happy to settle for one of us? She seems to like having both of us around."

"That was a fantasy, but it might not be what she wants in the long run."

Jai gestured dismissively with one hand, his eyes dark with anger. "I'm not stepping aside for you Garth. You'd never have even got her into bed if I hadn't been here. I didn't push you hard enough with Izzy, and you messed that up for everyone involved."

"Bastard." Garth's blood pumped way too fast.

"I've stuck by you all these years. If it hadn't been for me you probably would have messed it up again."

Garth had the urge to flatten him. "What, you're saying you stick by me because you stole Izzy from me?"

"I didn't steal her. She wanted you as well. It was like this, only you couldn't hack it."

"It wasn't like this. I want Faye, I care about her. She's just another leg over for you, another notch on the bedpost."

"Fuck you. You don't know how I feel about her. You never bother to ask how I feel about anything. It's all about you and your sensitive soul and having to deal with me and my approach to life."

"Excuse me for interrupting, but who the hell is Izzy?"

Garth swallowed his next rebuke and stared at Faye, who stood in the doorway. *God no.*

She looked a wreck. Her eyes were red rimmed and there were mascara streaks on her face—and she looked at him as if she thought he had a wife stashed away somewhere. Her face was flushed and her eyes were filled with hurt and mistrust.

Garth wanted to kick himself. He walked toward her, arms outstretched.

She put up her hands, blocking his approach. "You lied to me, you said you'd never shared another woman." Her voice sounded distraught. "At least I was honest about why I got involved! You two are in this because you have a competition going on about some woman you had in the past."

"That's not the case." Garth denied it vehemently.

Behind him, Jai backed him up, denying it too. "No, Faye, that's not the way it was at all."

Garth struggled to find the right thing to say, his mind reeling as he tried to work out how much and what exactly she'd heard. "We all came into this with history, with curiosity and different motives. We're just trying to make it work, decide who gets to see you."

As soon as he said that, Garth wanted to snatch the words back.

She glared at him. "So you think you can decide who I get to see." She made a disbelieving sound and shook her head. "Okay, maybe this was a bad idea after all. I need time out. I'll just get my things and I'll call for a taxi."

"Faye, please." Garth pleaded with her.

Jai stood back observing silently. When Garth looked his way, Jai shook his head. "Maybe we all need to step back and think about this with cool heads in the morning."

Faye was gathering her stuff together, shoving things into a bag. "I'll continue to do my research on Maud," she stated loudly, "and I'll be in touch regarding that matter as soon as I can."

She spoke in a businesslike manner, but her voice trembled and he could see that she was wiping away tears in between gathering her things. "I've had a hell of a time with her down there tonight, but I'm almost done now, I'm sure of it."

Garth's frustration with the turn of events grew. What had gone on down there? Most of all he couldn't believe Jai was going to let her walk out.

"See, it's easy for you to just let it go," he accused.

Jai stared at him, holding his gaze. "No, it isn't."

Garth's gut churned, because he could see it now—he could see it in Jai's eyes. He did care about her. He had been sincere about moving things forward with her. He could have probably taken her all for himself, but he'd been willing to share.

Chapter Thirteen

On Monday evening Faye sat in a taxi—which was queuing in the bumper-to-bumper early evening London traffic—on her way to Monica's reunion party at the Cumbernauld hotel, and she felt like a limp dishrag. All through the ride she mulled over the astonishing and emotional events of the last couple of days, and figured it was just as well the traffic crawled along. It might give her time to pull herself together before meeting her family.

It wasn't just the row with Garth and Jai, although that was the last straw. Peeling away Maud's layers had proved draining, because she'd fast grown to like her. The reason for Maud's afterlife existence had also left Faye horribly aware of how easy it was to make mistakes in life, and live to regret them. She'd been in no fit state for what followed.

The last thing she'd wanted was Jai and Garth fighting over her. They had a competitive dynamic, she was aware of that. What she didn't know was that she had fast become a big issue between them. They weren't just friends either. They were business partners, and that meant there was a lot at stake.

Guilt weighed heavily on her as she considered she might have screwed up their relationship for good, in the name of a bit of fun. The fact they'd apparently been in a similar situation before with another woman made it even worse. Garth was angry because of that, but it was no good reason to fight, and definitely no reason to carry on regardless of what her wishes might be.

By the time the taxi pulled up at Cumbernauld's her chaotic emotions were scarcely any more stable, but she felt a little more able to cope. Glancing up at the impressive façade of her sister's workplace, she vowed to live up to it. Once inside she made her way through the reception. Cumbernauld's was one of the most exclusive hotels in London and she'd always felt totally out of place meeting Monica and Holly there. That was why they usually opted to meet at a nearby Italian coffee house instead.

Out of the three of them, Monica was the one who had the most high-powered career, and whilst Faye looked up to her sister, she knew she could never work anywhere like this. Monica was the one with a business degree though, whereas Faye had a fine arts degree.

It didn't help that she hadn't changed into her nice dress for the event, as planned. What with one thing and another, there hadn't been time after work. She had meant to organise her outfit at lunchtime, but she'd spent the whole hour on the phone tracking information about adoption records. She'd made good progress there, so it was worth it. She'd hooked up with a woman who had a genuine interest in assisting people's enquiries, and she'd told Faye she'd look into it and get back to her. So, she was hopeful on that account, but she still wore her drainpipe jeans and a spider cobweb print top she'd made back in her print screen days at Art College. Not really fancy enough for Cumbernauld's, but it would have to do.

She hurried through the reception—where there were chandeliers hanging from the ceiling, marble pillars, and black and white tiles on the floors—and headed for the Byron bar. This meeting point was an elegant art deco cocktail bar, but it was much more pub-like than the formal reception area and the more subtle lighting put her a bit more at ease.

Almost immediately she saw Monica amongst friends. Her two lovers, Owen and Alec, hovered nearby chatting to other members of the group. Faye could sense how connected the three of them were even though they were able to socialise independently, and that left her in awe. Her attention went back to her sister.

FAYE'S SPIRIT

It'd been almost a year since Monica had gone away on business and they'd only seen her for a day at Christmas, which made this reunion a special moment. And she was home for several weeks. Faye was close to her sisters and it warmed and steadied her to see her eldest back home, especially so because she looked positively radiant. Monica had gained a little weight, which suited her. She'd been too lean, in Faye's opinion. Her posture was also much more relaxed than it used to be. Because Monica had psychic touch and experienced sexual history that way she'd tended to be a very isolated person. Not willing to joke around or touch and explore human contact in the normal way. Owen and Alec had changed that, and it showed. Faye felt incredibly grateful to them for bringing her sister such happiness. Emotion welled in her chest. It wasn't how she expected to react, and she chastised herself. But things had been fraught over the last twenty-four hours. Happy tears for Monica though, she realised, then wiped her eyes and smiled.

"Monica looks great," a woman nearby commented to her companion.

Faye took a sidelong glance. Five women were clustered together, and they all wore housekeeping uniforms. Monica used to be their supervisor before her promotion to hotel inspector for the Board of Directors.

"Yes, and she's got that glow," another of the women replied. "Hard to believe that bastard Flynn Elwood used to call her the Ice Queen," she added.

Mumbled agreements took place between the women.

Faye gave an internal sigh. Of course it might appear that way to outsiders. Monica's secret burden of psychic touch had made her a very aloof young woman. Her lovers had changed her forever. And it was obvious that Monica trusted them to care for her and protect her.

"Faye, are you all right?" Holly, the middle Evans' sister, had arrived at Faye's side and jolted her out of her thoughts.

"Yes. Just a bit overwhelmed at seeing Monica again."

"I know, and doesn't she look fabulous. I've never seen her so happy." Holly put her arm around Faye's shoulder then paused and glanced around. "I thought you were bringing someone?"

Faye's stomach knotted. "Sorry, I meant to let you know. It's just me. Not sure that's going to work out after all."

Holly studied her and Faye felt her cheeks flaming.

"It doesn't matter," she added quickly. That was a lie and it was futile, because Holly would sense it was a cover up.

"Do you want to talk about it?" Holly continued to study her. "We could grab two minutes to ourselves at some point."

Faye forced a smile. "No, it's okay, I just got ahead of myself as usual."

Stewart had joined them. Out of all the men her sisters were involved with, Faye secretly liked him the most. Why, she asked herself? Mostly it was his chilled attitude to sexuality. Jai had that in common with him. He was sporty, and he protected those he cared for. Like Garth. The qualities that she admired in Stewart she saw reflected in them. She did have a type, she supposed. And so many ways, Jai and Garth were right for her. *And in so many ways it was all wrong.*

"Hey, how are you doing?" Stewart kissed Faye on the cheek. "How's the ghost hunting business going?"

Stewart always asked. He seemed genuinely fascinated in both the paranormal work she did and her attempts to develop her own business. He was thinking of opening his own gym, and they exchanged ideas on the subject every time they met.

She was relieved to get off the subject of her love life. "Things are going better since one of my clients was very vocal about the work I'd done."

Stewart grinned. "I'll bear that in mind. Maybe I'll have to be personal trainer to someone famous, huh?"

"Sounds like a good strategy to me."

"You're on an investigation at the moment?" Holly asked.

"Yes, it's a fascinating ghost. She worked in a high class brothel in the sixties."

"Seriously?" Stewart rubbed his chin thoughtfully. "I hope you're documenting all these cases."

"I haven't as yet, but you're right. I'll definitely have to find time to make notes about Maud." Monica waved at them and headed over, and for a few minutes the three sisters were properly reunited.

Later in the event Owen called everybody's attention. "Many of you here might have guessed we invited you here in order to share this news with you." He had his arm around Monica, drawing her in against him.

Faye's breath hitched as she instinctively sensed what was coming next.

"Monica and I have been together for a year, and I'm delighted to share the news that she has graciously agreed to be my wife."

A moment's pause, then the room erupted into clapping and cheers and people began to step forward to congratulate the happy couple.

Faye's thoughts went immediately to Alec. What did he think of this development, was he happy with it? It didn't take long for Faye to spot him in the crowd. Tall, incredibly stylish and handsome, Alec Stroud stood out. And his attention was on his lovers. Faye didn't have to wonder for long, it was written all over him. He was happy. It made sense too. He'd been in a relationship with Owen before Monica met them. Owen was the dominant one, the one with the hugely public persona now that he had taken over the running of his father's hotel business. Alec would be at their side as he had been over the last year. Faye had no doubt about it.

He was approached a moment later by Holly and her lovers—Josh and Stewart. Stewart had a big grin on his face and leaned in to Alec to whisper something to him. Alec nodded. There was a natural understanding between them all. Envy reared inside Faye, followed closely by a tsunami of guilt. They were her sisters, and she was happy for them. She hated that she felt jealous, that she wanted that too. She recalled the moment Holly had phoned her to share what her relationship had become.

"I know it's going to sound kind of crazy," Holly had told her over the phone, "but we had a little ceremony on the beach last night. It was so pretty. Nothing official of course, but we bound ourselves to each other. I never thought it would work, but it has."

That had been three months earlier.

Faye had to swallow down the lump in her throat. Was it human nature to be so greedy, she wondered? She didn't shy away from it though. She wanted what they had. Three people supporting one another, being strong for each other when one or even two weren't so strong.

That's when it struck her with a dazzling blow that her relationship with Jai and Garth could never work. Seeing her two sisters this way meant the horrible truth dawned on her. Both their relationships were strong because the men were bisexual, the men were lovers too.

Her heart sank. She'd been so keen to experiment that it never occurred to her getting involved with two straight men might prove to be horribly complicated and impossible to manage. Garth and Jai had their own reasons for doing it, an old flame who had torn them apart. She was part of them working through a previous relationship. She'd hoped it had been more than that, but she had to face up to it and be realistic. They hadn't known each other long, she couldn't really expect more. Didn't mean she didn't crave it though. The resulting situation meant two old friends were now in turmoil, and she felt heartbroken and bereft.

It hit her so hard that she felt as if she wasn't really at the event—that she was outside it all, looking in. The cheerful chatter and laughter seemed distant to her, and she never felt more alone that she did at that moment. Alone with her problems—problems of her own making. Emotionally adrift and physically shaky, she took herself off to the ladies' cloakroom to check her mascara hadn't streaked. It was bad enough feeling like a lovelorn panda without looking like one too.

The austere facilities of the Cumbernauld's cloakroom didn't make her feel any more relaxed or comfortable. Normally she might try to enjoy the luxurious surroundings, but the cool marble and numerous mirrors only seemed to reflect her increasing isolation at that moment.

While she splashed her face Monica arrived, apparently hunting her down. Faye hurriedly adopted a smile.

Monica wasn't fooled. She hugged her, then very deliberately put her hands on Faye's shoulders and looked deep into her eyes.

Faye tried to pull away. Monica was touching her. This was bad news.

"Monica don't, please."

Monica wouldn't let her break the contact. "Holly said you were upset, and she thought it was something to do with a man." Monica's eyes widened. "It's not a man, it's two men?"

Sagging, Faye nodded. "I was stupid, I wanted to try it because you both had. I messed up, big time."

Monica squeezed her tightly then moved one hand to Faye's cheek, cupping her face. "Oh my, you have been busy. All this happened in the past few days?"

Faye sighed. Monica had a psychic window to her experiences because she had touched her. Faye didn't fight it because there was no point. There was nothing she could do about it. It took her right back to when she was sixteen years old and had headed off to a dubious party vowing to rid herself of her virginity. They had tracked her down. When they got her home Holly had given her a good telling off, and Monica had forced her to stand still while she found out exactly what had happened through touch. That time there wasn't much to learn. Not so this time. Having a big sister with psychometric skills didn't give her a lot of choice, but it also meant she didn't have to explain herself out loud.

"Oh, my poor poppet. You're really feeling it." Monica drew Faye into her arms, hugging her.

She hadn't heard her sister used the term "poor poppet", for many years. She would usually retort that she wasn't a poor poppet and stomp off. This time she didn't. Instead, she melted into the embrace, savouring the familiarity, the comfort.

"Yes. I've fallen fast. Very silly of me. Don't get me wrong, I went in with my eyes open and I was only looking for a bit of fun, I wanted to know what it would be like."

Monica drew back and looked at her again. "And you thought they'd experienced a threesome before?"

Faye nodded. "As you can probably tell, it's complicated. There was a woman in the past that they both cared for, and I think maybe I've brought bad memories for them."

Her sister studied her with those wise eyes of hers.

"If it's any excuse, I like them both. A lot."

"Of course you do. It would be hard to manage them otherwise." Monica laughed softly.

"It's different to you and Holly. They are business partners, but they are both straight. They're friends and I feel as if I have come between them now."

Monica frowned. She still had one hand loosely around Faye's shoulder, so her information was coming in from both sources—what Faye said, and what she could see for herself. "Everybody went into this willingly?"

Faye nodded. "But now they're arguing about which one of them gets to keep seeing me." Her voice wavered badly, her emotions getting the better of her. "And then I heard mention of this woman they were both involved with."

"It seems as if it happened quite quickly and things have got fraught and complicated now?"

Again Faye nodded, dabbing at her eyes she did so. "It was just a bit of playful sex to begin with."

Monica finally broke the physical contact. "This relationship may or may not work out, but walking away from them won't help sort it out, will it?"

"I know. It's too soon. I had to get away because I could see it had become a big issue between them. I didn't want to ruin the bond they had."

"I can understand that. Nothing in life is simple. Even with a couple, there has to be compromise and sometimes that can be really hard. That's what a relationship needs, investment of the self. When there are three of you, obviously there has to be three-way compromises. Sharing problems makes it easier, but it's always more complicated when there are three. What you see of Holly and I and our relationships is really the end result, the rewards."

"I do remember what you both went through, you told me."

Monica smiled and nodded. "You were always at the end of the phone for us. And now you must let us be there for you. Promise you won't bottle it up?"

She nodded. Monica reached into her pocket and handed over a tissue.

Faye took the hint, looked at herself in the mirror and used the tissue to scrub under her eyelids where her mascara had streaked.

"I have to get back out there now," Monica said. "Will you be all right?"

Faye looked at her sister's reflection in the mirror. "Yes. Thanks."

"It's not easy, but if they can come to terms with sharing you and you have come into this as three single people, talking it through is the way forward." With that final encouragement, Monica left.

Faye frowned at herself in the mirror. Yes, she'd done the wrong thing shouting her mouth off then marching out on them. But they had been at each other's throats. She couldn't bear it. If that's what she'd done to them, it was better she ended it and quickly. Monica was right, she couldn't just run away, but she could nip it in the bud now.

Stupid, stupid woman. Sadness swamped her and she wished she'd never kicked the relationship off in the first place. It was wrong, bound to end in trouble. Nevertheless she couldn't bring herself to regret the crazy few days she'd spent with them and the sexual experimentation, but she did regret causing tension and bad feeling between the two men. When she reached for the phone and glanced at the screen, something she often did to comfort and distract herself, she discovered both Garth and Jai had inundated her with text messages and voicemail.

It was with an even more weighty sinking feeling that she realised she was going to have to work her way through them, in order to check to see if her contact at the adoption agency records department had left a message.

There it was. She played the message and pulled out her pen and notepad to scribble down the details. Maud's son had been adopted by a Mr and Mrs Butterfield. They'd kept the Christian name given to him by his natural mother, and he'd been brought up in Bromsgrove in Kent as Harry Butterfield, one of five adopted children in a large catholic family.

"Bingo." Faye smiled, even though her eyes smarted. If she could find Harry Butterfield, she could move forward. That meant she could try to resolve Maud's issue and finish her work for Garth. It also meant she could attempt to tidy up the mess she had created with Jai and Garth, bringing them back to the sound friends and colleagues they had been before, and then they could all get back to their regularly scheduled lives.

It should have made her feel better, so why did it make her feel so bad?

Chapter Fourteen

"It's a message from Faye?"

Garth nodded.

"What, what did she say?"

Garth stared down at his phone, scanning the message.

I am trying to find Maud's son. She gave him up for adoption and needs to know what happened to him. Let's just take a step back while I do this. Please give me some space to think. I promise I'll try to sort things out with Maud then we'll talk about what went down between the three of us. I want you to be okay with each other, like you were before I met you.

"She said... Oh, read it yourself." He handed the phone over.

Jai paced the floor. Garth forced himself to watch. Jai, Mr Cool, would normally laugh something like this off. Instead he walked back and forth, his eyebrows drawn down and his expression serious.

"Wants us to be okay, what the..." He lifted his hands, and for a moment Garth thought he was going to throw the phone across the room.

Instead he drew it back and went over the message again.

A weight settled on Garth's shoulders, adding to the one that was already there. Guilt that he hadn't realised Jai was every bit as involved with this as he was, and regret at the way he'd handled it.

"The rest I get, but…what the fuck? We weren't any different with each other than we were before Faye came long. We're always arguing. That's just the way we function."

Garth nodded. "I know that, you know that, but Faye doesn't know that."

"True, I suppose."

"You know what she said to me, she said we're like an old married couple, and she was right, that's exactly what we are."

Jai looked kind of shocked by the revelation and so he might, considering how it undermined his cool image.

Garth resisted commenting.

"Let's go to her place, come on." Jai fronted up to him.

"No." Garth stood up. "She's asked for space. If we don't give her that now, she'll definitely think we don't respect her. She'll dump us for good. I want more than a few days of kinky sex. If you want to walk away I understand that, but know this, I don't, and I won't."

"You know I don't want to walk away."

"It's about what she wants now."

Garth stared at Jai. Part of him wanted his old friend to declare that there were plenty of other fish in the sea and to waltz out. Then he'd be there to pick up the pieces with Faye, he'd make it right. God knows he would give all he had to make it right. But he'd had time to think, and part of him also knew that if Jai went there would be a massive hole in the relationship, one that he might not be able to fill no matter how hard he tried. He had no idea how this was going to work out. The bottom line was that Faye had to have her say, or she'd walk away forever.

Jai's head lowered, and he nodded. "You're right buddy, you are right."

When he eventually met Garth's stare there was a searching look in Jai's eyes that made Garth prickle with tension. Doubts assailed him, but he felt alive, more alive than he ever had. He'd always wanted goals, something to fight for, and now he really had the chance—*they* really had it. "Good things are always worth working hard for."

He closed on Jai and put his hand on Jai's shoulder. "She'll come back, she said she would." How strange it was, he realised, that he was comforting Jai, the one who normally led from the rear. "We'll talk then."

Jai stared at him, then humour briefly flashed in his eyes. "Promise?"

Garth grinned. "Arsehole."

"Yeah, and you."

It took Faye less than two days to track down Maud's son. She considered that good going. It also gave her time to calm down about the mess she'd got herself in with Jai and Garth. Calm down she did, but somehow that only made her ache for them all the more. Focusing on the task she had to complete, the promise she had to fulfil for Maud, was the only thing that kept her moving forward. If it wasn't for that goal, she'd have been staring at the walls in her flat thinking of them right around the clock.

Thank goodness for Harold Butterfield, or Harry, as Maud had called him.

Luckily there were only two men by the name of Harold Butterfield in the correct age group, and the first one she found turned out to be a false lead. That only left one, the Harry Butterfield who lived in a village in Kent and ran a small bespoke shoe manufacturing company located in the east end of London. This was Maud's son, and the notes had shown that he'd been informed that he'd been adopted, but hadn't pursued it. That didn't bode well.

Faye opted to visit him at work, to keep this separate from his family. His business was located in an old mill in Shoreditch. She looked up at the building as she approached and it made her think how much Garth and Jai would love the place. Damn them. They'd got in her head—under her skin and in her blood—and now every funny thought she had and every building she looked at she wanted to share with them. She wanted to ask them about the architecture, loving the way they had educated her about things she'd never even thought about before she met them, just a few days before.

The place had been modernised internally, but kept many of the original features. How odd it was that he'd started his business here in the east end, where his mother's line had come from. It was a coincidence. No doubt he got good terms on the site during the regeneration years, but it felt poignant to Faye nonetheless. Such was her own emotional involvement now, an involvement she knew had grown too deep, but she couldn't stop it and didn't try.

He hadn't moved far from his beginnings, but Harry had done well for himself in life. If she didn't get any further than this, she had that news for Maud. But Faye wanted to give her more than that.

She braced herself and stepped into the building. An austere, mature receptionist looked up from her keyboard as Faye entered. "How can I help you?"

"I wondered if I could possibly see Mr Harry Butterfield?"

"Is he expecting you?"

Thankfully, he was there. One bit of weight lifted from her shoulders. That had been her first concern. "No, he isn't."

"Can I ask what it is concerning?"

"It's a personal matter."

The receptionist eyed her warily. "Mr Butterfield will not see you if your intention is to try to sell him something."

"I'm not here to sell him anything. It's a personal issue that I need to discuss with him."

The receptionist rose to her feet. "Take a seat. I'll see if he is available."

"Thank you."

Faye didn't sit down. Instead she paced back and forth in front of the reception desk with her fingers meshed together. Silently she chanted *please please, please let me in.*

The receptionist returned and ushered Faye in.

Harry Butterfield was a business man in his late forties, and he appeared to be a down to earth type of man. Tall, with a shaved head and determined looking, he had the kind of energy about him that successful people often did. He wore a smart shirt and tie, but with the sleeves rolled up.

He had an intelligent, sharp look in his expression and Faye warmed to him immediately, because it did remind her of Maud and that assessing look she wore sometimes. It made Faye eager to share her knowledge, even though he regarded her rather warily when she announced she had a personal reason for requesting a meeting, and she knew this might present a few hurdles.

"Thank you for seeing me, I know you're a busy man." She took the seat he gestured to in front of his desk. The office was practical and business like, located right in the hub of activity in the warehouse where his workers produced footwear that sold worldwide. She stored every image away for Maud.

"As long as you're not trying to sell me anything." He smiled but there was a warning there. He wasn't a man who wasted time. He took his seat and gave her his full attention.

"No, I assure you I'm not. I'm here because I've been hired by someone to find out the history of their building, and the people who worked there. In the course of my investigation I've uncovered some of your family history."

Harry froze.

"Your birth mother worked in the building, and...and I know her name, as well as your father's."

The approachable look evaporated immediately. It was as if shutters came down over his eyes. He rose to his feet. "Miss Evans, I granted you a meeting because I thought you came here to ask about whether there were any jobs going in the factory."

Faye nodded quickly. "I assure you I haven't come to sell you anything. I'm working for someone else researching the history of their home and I have revealed knowledge that might be important to you."

"It's not important to me," he retorted, his voice growing louder. He paused as if gathering himself.

"It never has been and it never will be," he added in a more contained tone. "I think you should leave."

She'd known it would be awkward, but for a moment she really thought he was going to throw her out. He began to walk around the desk.

She rose to her feet. "Please, hear me out."

He shook his head. He really didn't want to know. "You've got some spin on this, you're going to bait me and then sell me the rest, but you're wasting your time because I'm really not interested in the bastards who gave me away."

She felt as if she'd been physically slapped in the face. This man had years of silent anger in him, that was obvious, but she had to get tough because she couldn't let Maud down.

"I have no agenda." Her heart beat hard in her chest. "Your mother's name was Maud Radisson. She worked in Highgate as a cook. Your father was an Italian delivery driver called Paulo Albertina. He worked in London briefly, in the early sixties."

Harry stopped and rocked on his heels. Now it was him that looked as if he'd been slapped in the face. Naming them had hit him hard.

"They met when he delivered delicatessen supplies from Fortnum and Mason to the place where she worked, but he went home, to Italy, and she found out about you after that, when she was alone."

He stared at her in disbelief.

Grasping the opportunity, she cleared her throat and nodded. Quickly unfolding the papers that she had kept folded in her hand, documents that she'd picked up from the adoption agency on her way over here, she laid them flat on the desk and gestured. As she did, she noticed that her hand shook. "Take a look at the paperwork and I'll explain why I am here."

Harry Butterfield stared down at the pages.

Scarcely able to look, Faye forced herself to stay quiet, and glanced away. In the background she could hear the rhythmic noise of the machinery in the factory beyond. Here in the office all was still, bar the motes of dust that shifted and floated on the atmosphere, visible in the wintry sunlight pouring in at the window. Like time marching on, filling people's lives with emotions, bringing happiness and tragedy, hope and loss, along the way.

It was almost as if Harry forgot she was there. He was well and truly captured by their names, by the proof they really had lived, and loved. He reached for his glasses, picked up the pages, and slowly sank back into his chair as he glanced over the paperwork.

There was a chance. Faye willed him to open up, to talk to her. Even if he refused to go further, she would be able to tell Maud about him, how well he'd done, what a fine man she'd brought into this world. That was what Maud needed to know, her every instinct told her that.

As Faye took her seat as well, emotion welled inside her. How she wished she could have Maud here with her, to see him. She recalled Maud saying how tall and striking Paulo was. This man was the product of their brief love affair and

Faye took the opportunity to look at him and memorise his features so that she could describe him to Maud.

"Maud Radisson?" He said her name aloud, a note of reluctant curiosity in his voice. He stared down at the paperwork, reading and rereading the details of his birth and adoption, and eventually leant back in his chair.

Faye took this to indicate some level of acceptance. She gave him another few moments of reflection, before she edged it forward.

"Did you ever investigate yourself?" She asked the question tentatively, knowing that he could flip back at any moment. Had he now accepted her visit?

"No. Not officially. I went to a good family. I was one of the lucky ones. I thought about it a lot once my parents told me, but I sincerely believed that my birth parents, whoever they were, obviously did not want me to be part of their lives. Their decision…her decision, I guess." Betrayal shone in his eyes for the briefest of moments. Then it was gone. "If my mother had come to me, I would have been willing to listen, but I didn't want to be the poor bastard turning up unwanted on someone's doorstep, especially if they had perhaps started a new life, a happy one without me."

Faye nodded. It made sense, although she knew that he had to have quashed some deep emotion and curiosity to arrive at that understanding of his situation.

The time had come for her to bring up the next reason for her visit. "Well, in effect, it is your mother who has sent me to find you."

This was the really awkward part. It had been hard enough revealing to the poor man that she knew about his origins, and now she had to tell him why and how.

His eyebrows lifted. "She's still alive?"

Faye detected the faintest hint of hope in his tone. "Alas, no." She took a deep breath. "I've come here because I am a psychic and I have encountered the lingering ghost of your birth mother."

Harry Butterfield stared at her as if she were insane.

"I realise how difficult that is for you to take in, but it is genuinely the case and if you're willing, I can tell you the details I have learnt about your early life." Faye offered a sympathetic nod, attempting to indicate her understanding.

"I don't believe in ghosts." At first he shook his head, then he stared out of the window for a few moments.

Faye took a deep breath and began explaining. It was no easy task to put forward a simple and accessible account. The swinging Sixties, the girl who fell for the deliveryman, a baby that she couldn't have afforded to bring up, one she was talked into putting up for adoption. The reality of that harsh adoption process and the sadness left behind in Maud's life.

As the story unfolded, Harry Butterfield alternately frowned, then shook his head and touched his fingers to his forehead, his eyes reflecting the myriad of emotions he'd been forced to feel. It was so much to take in.

"What you are telling me is difficult for me to believe because I had no knowledge of my beginnings in life," Harry Butterfield stated, "but this business of a ghost. It's beyond the realms of anything that I have ever encountered." He frowned heavily, his face becoming more familiar to her by the moment, resembling as it did his mother's features.

Faye nodded. "I know how far-fetched this probably seems to you, but I have the talent as a medium and I can often communicate with the spirits of those who have gone before in order to the find out why they linger. I was commissioned by a client to investigate the presence in a building he purchased and restored. I communicated with the spirit and I found the sadness that kept her connected to our world relates to the fact she had to give her child away at birth, and that she never knew what happened to him."

She tried to keep her voice as steady as possible, and as soothing. It was a skill she learned young in life, first dealing with her sister Monica's dramatic childhood, where she was often bullied and ridiculed by other kids when they learned about her psychometric abilities. She'd fast learned to grow patient when her own talents developed, trying to explain to people around her that she was not talking to an invisible friend, that she was communicating with a spirit.

"Would you be willing to come to my employer's house? You would learn a little more about your origins, and it would be a great comfort to the spirit of your departed mother if you would."

"This is too strange." He put his elbows on the armrests of his chair and steepled his fingers beneath his chin. Luckily for Faye, he was a cautious man, and had not thrown her out on her ear when she'd arrived to his workplace requesting a meeting. She had to be every bit as sensitive to his needs as she was to Maud's. She couldn't push him into doing something he didn't want to do, because of her loyalty to Maud.

He wasn't sure though, and she worked on instinct, rising to her feet. "I'll leave you to think about it. Here's my card." She put her business card down on his desk. "Call me if you would like to visit the place where your parents met."

Chapter Fifteen

Faye didn't have to work at the shop on Thursdays, so she was at home when Harry rang—and feeling very sorry for herself she was too. It was far too easy to spend the time brooding about her love life. She'd even tried to watch the footage they'd captured on Saturday, but it made her even more unhappy. Not to mention desperately aroused.

But now Harry wanted to go to the house, and he'd agreed to meet her in his car later that day. It got her out of bed and into the shower, and after she'd dressed, she braced herself to call Garth.

When the phone was answered, Faye quickly interrupted Garth's outpouring of concern and enquiries after her wellbeing.

"Garth, I've met with Maud's son, Harry Butterfield."

Garth paused and she sensed the tension at the other end of the line. He was trying to be well behaved. Thankfully.

"I wondered if I could bring him to your offices this afternoon before it gets dark?"

"Yes, of course you can, any time. How did he take it?"

The very sound of his voice made her ache to be in his arms again. It also made her want to tell him off for attempting to lay down the law with Jai without even consulting her. "It's been rather a steep learning curve, as you might imagine. I suggested if we have a walk around place where his mother met his father, it will benefit both him and Maud."

"And he's willing?" Disbelief sounded in his voice.

"He wasn't at first, but he's had a change of heart. Curiosity, I think."

"Strike while the iron's hot, ay?" He sounded a bit more hopeful.

Was that because he'd get to see her, too? "Yes, I thought it'd be good to do this straight away, before he changes his mind again."

"This will help Maud?"

"I think so, and then I'll have completed the job." Silence reigned, so Faye quickly filled it. "If you could arrange for the door to be open at three so there's still light in the yard…and it would also be very helpful if the downstairs area was vacant."

She paused to allow that to sink in. The reasons for asking him not be around were twofold. She didn't need the distraction, neither did Harry or Maud. More than that, she wasn't ready to deal with him just yet. She wanted to wrap up her work obligation before having it out with them. When she cleared the air, she would walk away. "I promise I'll speak to you before I leave, but we need to spend a while there in peace."

"I see." Garth's response seemed guarded, and she sensed he was hurt, but he didn't really have a choice. He'd hired her to encourage Maud to move on and that's exactly what Faye was doing.

Huntington House, as the place had been known when Harry was born there, was busy. Harry had parked up on the other side of the road and both he and Faye watched as people went in and out of the building.

"It now belongs to the local council and it's a designated family centre."

Harry nodded at her comment but continued to stare at the building.

Faye could only guess at the troubled thoughts seeing the place might bring. "Quite different than when it was a convent centre for adoptions."

"Yes, it would have been a shielded environment, I imagine." He looked at her then, and she saw that the more genial personality he'd exhibited when she first met him had returned. "Thank you for this. My wife pointed out to me that you had no need to go to quite such lengths for your client. It made me think."

"I didn't have to, but I wanted to. Your mother's spirit lingers because she has regrets, because she never knew what happened to you. But she thought she could watch from afar, or at least enquire about your upbringing. Because she died within six months, that need was never fulfilled."

Harry reached for the ignition. "Come on then, let's do it."

As she gave him directions, she sent a text message to Garth stating they were on their way over. Her finger hovered over the send button. Once she'd shown Harry around and encouraged Maud to take the experience she offered, she would have to deal with her own issues.

Nerves had got the better of her and she felt dizzy at the thought of the next couple of hours. Fretting over Maud and Harry, then Garth and Jai. Staring out of the passenger window, she said a rare prayer, wishing for common sense and good luck in her dealings with all four of them.

Jai prayed for patience.

Garth paced up and down the sitting area of his flat, occasionally pausing to throw Jai annoyed glances. Jai was determined not to leave, even though Faye had stated they shouldn't be here at all. Besides, they both knew they had to get Faye alone in order to apologise. They couldn't risk her leaving before they had a chance to speak to her. They'd freaked her out over the Izzy thing, and—if nothing else—they had to straighten out that misunderstanding. Of course Jai wanted a lot more than that, both of them did.

He tried to ignore Garth's persistent pacing back and forth and stared out of the front window of the top floor flat, peering up and down the busy street, watching out for Faye's arrival.

Just then he saw a flash of red as she rounded the corner and her hair blew out on the breeze. By her side walked a tall, smartly dressed bloke with a shaved head. "Here they come. Quickly, let's get down to the second floor landing. We should be able to hear from there."

Garth stared across his living room, incredulous. "No way, you can't be serious?"

Jai glared at him. He needed Garth on the ball. "Are you kidding?"

"She asked for privacy, and I for one want to give her that much respect."

"What, to make up for the lack of respect we showed her last time she was here?" Jai gave him a deliberately accusing look.

"Do you have to be quite so grating?"

His comment really did push Garth's buttons. Jai had to laugh. "We're over that now, we know where we stand with each other. Neither of us wants to miss out with Faye. We both know what we have to do when we talk to her, right?"

Garth nodded.

"Look," Jai added, "aren't you curious about what will happen down there?" All three of them were invested in their resident spirit and the outcome of Faye's investigations. Neither of them could deny that, even if right at that moment they had more important things on their mind.

Garth sighed. "Yes, but it's more important that we don't rattle Faye any more than we have already."

"We've agreed, we'll offer to roll things back to where we were on Sunday and just chill with that." Jai gave a gesture of peace with his hands, striding toward the door to the landing as he did so.

As he got out there the sound of the front door clicking shut reached him. He leaned over the railing. The narrow niche that ran down the centre of the building allowed a glimpse of the hallway from above. He'd always considered it perfect for spying, but never had he thought how important it would be to him until now.

Faye walked into view.

His grip tightened on the railing.

For a moment he felt frozen to the spot, the sight of her confirming everything he'd avoided facing up to. Originally it had been about sexual thrill. But now that he saw her again he knew that he cared for her every bit as much as Garth did. Even though he recognised how much he felt for her, he also knew that if she asked him to leave her and Garth alone, he would have to.

Right at that moment, she looked up and met his stare.

Jai didn't have time to back off, even if he'd wanted to, and he didn't want to.

Faye locked eyes with him.

His stomach knotted, and for the first time since he was a kid he didn't feel sure of what was going on around him.

Faye. He silently spoke to her.

Her eyes flickered at him for the longest moment. Then she looked away and he realised she was looking for Garth. Glancing over his shoulder, he gestured at the big guy, calling him over.

Garth hovered by the door to his living space, unsure.

Jai waved at him again.

Mercifully Garth moved, but by the time he'd got there, she'd walked on and out of view. "Too late," Jai whispered. "She knows we're up here though."

"What the fuck?" Garth glared at him.

"Chill. She expected it."

Garth clicked into gear, accepting that, and joined Jai in peering over the railing.

Her voice echoed up the stairs, barely discernible, but distinctly her all the same.

Garth visibly relaxed. "It's so good to hear her voice in the house again."

Jai nodded.

Garth turned his way. "I'm falling in love with her, you do know that?"

Jai took a deep breath before he replied. "Yup, I know that."

Chapter Sixteen

When they arrived at the house Faye had already been a mess of emotions. Tremulous hope that this would bring some closure for Maud was at the forefront of her mind, closely followed by managing the situation for Harry in the best way possible. To some extent she was going to have to wing it and see how things panned out. The most important thing was to try and draw Maud out as soon as possible.

Then, as she walked up the steps it reminded her of the day she'd arrived there, only a week before, and everything that had happened in the relationship with Jai and Garth came flooding back.

Once she had dealt with the first issue then came her own problematic love life. Why was it easier to focus on the first issue? She had been trying to keep it all in perspective, when she instinctively looked up and saw Jai.

It left her shaky, because just seeing him made her realise how much she'd missed him. She had to stop herself running up the stairs and throwing herself into his arms while telling him off for being there.

"This is an impressive building."

Harry's voice brought her back to the moment and the first job on her list.

"It is, take a look at the reception area." She gestured then followed him into the reception.

"Crikey," he exclaimed when he saw the glass wall and the inner workings of the architect workshop. His reaction made her smile.

Stepping close to the glass division he peered through it, taking an obvious interest in how it all worked. "I'll keep these guys in mind if I ever need an architect."

FAYE'S SPIRIT

Faye noticed that the reception area hadn't altered since she'd first arrived here. The cushions were still wrapped in cellophane and boxed computer equipment went unopened. The brass plaque still sat in its packaging. Surely they should have been working on that for their grand opening the following week?

"Yes, they seem to be good at what they do," she responded, vaguely, and tried to concentrate on Maud, sending out a psychic call. It would be hard. For a start she'd never seen Maud surface this early in the day, and she hadn't been back to keep Maud in the picture. *Please, please, Maud. I haven't abandoned you, I have found your son and he is with me.*

"Hard to imagine it as it would have been in the sixties." Harry had turned to look at her.

Faye snapped into action and nodded. "Apparently it was quite a sumptuous building. Let me take you to the kitchen where your birth mother used to work doing the catering. There've been fewer changes there but you can still imagine what it would have looked like back then."

She led the way back out into the hall, and into the kitchen. "It's a bit more relaxed in here."

She stood close to the sink and looked out into the yard as Maud had done so many times on repeat. "This is where your mother and father met. He did deliveries and pulled his van into this yard outside."

Harry stood in the middle of the kitchen for a moment fixed to the spot, as if trying to take it in. Then he stepped closer and looked out of the window.

Faye went to the back door and unlocked it. She opened it and went out onto the steps that led down to the yard area. "The place is fenced in now, whereas in previous years it was open onto the lane that runs along the back of the houses here, for deliveries."

Harry joined her, and she noticed he had his hands in his pockets and looked slightly awkward. Did he sense something, or was it just the unusual nature of the situation? After a moment he stepped into the yard, pacing across it to look back up at the house.

Faye took the chance to go back into the kitchen. "Maud Radisson, please come, please show yourself to me! Maud, please!" She couldn't bear thinking about how awful it would be if Harry left before Maud arrived.

She went to the sink and clutched the edge of it with both hands, observing as Harry moved around the yard. Then she felt it, a rush of psychic energy that was so strong it shook her innards.

Maud was at her side. "Where've you been? The men have been in such a state without you. I thought you'd gone forever, so did they and they've been worried sick."

Faye saw the genuine concern in Maud's expression. It touched her deeply, and once again she wished that she could hug her, hold her, and interact with her properly. "Don't worry, they'll stop fighting soon. I've come back to right that wrong."

"It's not wrong. They don't think it was wrong. They've missed you so much."

Maud had been listening in on their discussions. Faye longed to know what had been said, but it would only make things harder for her if she knew. She lifted her hands and spread her fingers apart. Maud stared at them then cautiously lifted her own. The psychic energy between them gave Faye a jolt, like a small electric shock.

"Thank you for caring."

"But Faye, it's you they want."

Faye jolted again, and this time it was more powerful. Maud had pushed that notion out there with enormous effort, and it assaulted Faye's senses. Maud wanted her to know, to feel what she had discovered.

It wedged in Faye's chest, an ache, a sense of longing for completeness. She'd grown to care about them, and Maud was trying to tell her how they cared too, but Faye didn't have the time to think about it. Any second now Harry would walk back into the room, and she had to warn Maud and prepare her for that moment. Her own issues would wait until this was done.

"Hush, please, I have something important to tell you and I must be quick." She locked eyes with Maud, pleading with her to stay calm. "I've brought a visitor to see the house." She nodded her head at the window. "I found him. That's your son, Harry."

Maud stared at the window, her head bobbing as she leaned right over the sink to get a better look. When she caught sight of him she pulled back and her hands covered her face. Her eyes glistened, the psychic energy coming off her quickly making Faye feel quite dizzy. Faye felt the shock, the disbelief, then the growing intrigue.

Maud reached for Faye as if by instinct, her ghostly fingertips leaving a maddening trail of static electricity down Faye's arm. "He's coming into the kitchen."

"I don't know if he will see you or not, but I'll keep him here talking for a while so that you can see him."

"He looks like Paolo," Maud whispered.

"I wondered if that was the case." Faye nodded at her reassuringly and as soon as she heard Harry entering the kitchen, she turned his way.

Harry looked only at her.

Faye's heart sank. There'd only been a small chance that he might have been able to see Maud. No one else had. Not properly, like she did. But still Faye hoped that they might have been able to have a proper exchange.

"Do you feel anything?" she asked tentatively. "Any connection to the place?"

"To be honest, no." He gave her a brief courteous smile, as if he secretly thought she was bonkers. "But I'm glad I came."

"He really does look like Paolo," Maud said and smiled.

She looked so pleased, so happy and relieved, that Faye thanked her lucky stars and whoever else had been involved in helping to make this work. There had been so many elements of it left to chance. Harry could have emigrated to Australia. He might have been on holiday this week. But no, because he was meant to come here, she was never more sure of anything in that moment.

She noticed that Harry looked thoughtful. "Are you all right?"

"Yes. It's just so weird. The information that was missing all my life is now there, but it's still hard for me to take it on board."

"I'm sure it'll be easier once you've had time to process it all." She kept an eye on Maud as she spoke.

Harry nodded. "So you say they met here, that he delivered here?" He stared back at the door where the steps went down to the yard.

"Yes. They would have chatted right here, where we're standing."

Maud had once again covered her mouth with one hand and crept across the room, staring at her son with tear filled eyes.

She didn't seem to expect him to see her, but she'd existed many years in spirit form and it was only Faye who had. There was some comfort in that for Faye, but still she wished he could see Maud's spirit, or feel her. Maybe it was better that he didn't, though.

It was the oddest situation that Faye had ever been in, since she first communicated with ghosts all those years ago as a child. None of the investigative work she'd done over the last year had turned out like this, like some sort of long lost family reunion that only one half of the family was aware of.

The massive swirl of emotion that she got from Maud was making it hard for her to remember her planned moves, and she forced herself to focus. "I think what your mother needed to know most of all was that she had put you on a good path. She never knew. Perhaps if she had lived longer she could have gone to the adoption agency and enquired after you. I believe that might have been her intention."

Harry frowned. "Will she know now?"

"Yes, I'm sure she will."

"I've never thought about how she felt or what happened to her. As a teenager, when my parents told me, it was all about the fact that someone didn't care enough to keep me. Then I just blanked it out. Now that it's falling into place I feel differently. I know that if it was my own kids I'd want to know how they were doing in life."

"I think she'd be proud of you Harry, you've had a good life and that's all she wanted for you."

"Yes, I have."

Maud glanced at Faye and Maud nodded quickly, tears spilling down her cheeks as she did so.

"I was unsure about this, about coming here," Harry added. "I'm glad that I did. Thank you."

Faye felt her throat tighten. The time had come for him to leave and she didn't know how Maud would take it. "You'll be on your way now," she said, forcing Maud to acknowledge it.

Maud reacted. Reaching out, she moved her hand as if to touch her son then drew back. Harry shifted his shoulders and glanced over to the place where Maud stood.

Faye's breath caught. He put out his hand to Faye.

She forced herself to act, took his hand and shook it. "I have to speak with the owners of the property. I'll be sure they know your name, and if you want to come and visit the place again they'll instruct their receptionist to show you around during working hours."

"I don't think that will be necessary, but I appreciate it."

Faye showed him out and gave a deep sigh of relief after she'd waved him off and shut the front door behind him.

She looked down the hallway.

Maud had stayed in the kitchen, and the psychic energy that came from that direction was like a floating cloud of pulsating emotion. She glanced at the staircase. The distant sound of a mumbled conversation drew her closer to the bottom of the stairs.

She looked up and saw them both there. Grasping the polished banister she lifted her eyebrows and looked at them accusingly.

"Should we come down?" Garth asked.

She could hardly tell him off about being in his own house, but she wasn't ready to speak to them yet. She shook her head. "I'll come up when I'm ready. I'm still on Maud time at the moment."

Somehow, taking control and putting them on hold made her feel a bit more together. They both nodded but didn't move, continuing to lean over the railing and stare down at her expectantly.

"Boy, this is going to be a long day," she murmured to herself as she headed back to kitchen.

"Why didn't you go to them?" Maud asked as Faye dropped onto a chair.

"They can wait. We've got unfinished business. I want to tell you everything I learned about your son."

Maud's eyes widened.

Her pleasure lifted Faye's mood. Part of it was procrastination, because she was dreading going up there and saying her goodbyes. It had to be done, but right now she was all about doing her job and doing it well.

"Congratulations Maud, you're a grandmother."

"Grandchildren?" Maud's jaw dropped.

"Four times over, apparently."

Faye went through everything, describing Harry's office and his business, what she knew of his adopted parents and his own wife and family.

"Thank you, a million times thank you," Maud said, as Faye finally came to the end of her mental notes.

Maud's aura seemed to glow and yet she also seemed diminished. Her spirit presence was already fading. "You've given me the one thing I have wished for all these years."

Faye had one more question. "It wasn't Paolo who broke your heart."

Maud shook her head. "I told you it wasn't what you'd think."

"You didn't want give up the baby."

"No, I didn't. I was plagued by regret the moment they took him from my arms, until now." Maud stared at Faye, and Faye knew what she was trying to say.

"I was thinking about him the night of the crash. I wondered where he was, if he was warm enough, if he'd been fed. I hit a patch of black ice, and then—when I found myself like this, in limbo—I thought I'd never know if he was warm enough, and how he fared. But now I do know, because you came here."

Faye swallowed down the lump in her throat. "I'm glad I helped you, Maud."

"Now you must help yourself." Maud nodded her head upwards. "Give them a chance to explain themselves, and you won't regret it." A faint smile appeared on her face. "Go on, shoo!"

Then she faded away and was gone.

Chapter Seventeen

As soon as Faye walked through the door, they both started talking at the same time, then shushed each other to silence, then began talking to her at the same time again.

The words came at her in a rush, and she couldn't take any of it in.

"Be quiet!" She waved her hands.

They went quiet. She dropped onto the sofa. "Maud saw her son."

"Faye?" Jai stared at her, looking for a response.

"I'm sorry, tough day at the office." She felt the mad urge to laugh. They were both looking at her as if they were in suspended animation. "Just give me a chance to say what I have to say."

She took a deep breath and stood up. "First of all, I want to apologise for walking out the other night. I couldn't handle it. I'd been through the ringer with Maud that night."

"I felt awful about that," Garth said, "when I realised. The timing was poor."

"I overheard what you were saying and it made me wonder about your motivation for getting involved with me." They both opened their mouths to speak. Faye put up a hand. "Let me finish. Then, when I got some distance on this, I realised that the past is the past and I had no right to get upset about it. My main reason for being upset and regretting this is that I made you two fight, and hated myself for that."

They both shook their heads.

She paused, but she'd prepared her speech and she had to get through it before she blubbed. "You have a wonderful friendship and I refuse to jeopardise that." Now for the really hard bit. "I didn't want us to part the way we did, with bad feelings. I came up here to clear the air, and to thank you for a wonderful weekend. Please don't fight because of me. Don't let last weekend come between you and the bond you have in your friendship and your work. I need to know that you two will be okay."

They both stared at her as if she were mad.

She was getting that a lot lately.

Jai spoke first. "We'll be okay, but we need you to stay in our lives."

"Yes, we will be okay," Garth agreed, "but we'll be better than okay if we still have you."

"I can't risk—"

"Faye!" Garth pushed his fingers through his hair. Tension throbbed in the atmosphere around him. "Faye, please believe me, you were our motivation for getting involved. There was someone a long time ago, it was nothing like what I…we, feel for you. The opportunity had been there to have a threesome in the past, but I didn't want it then."

"No, he didn't. Not the way he wanted you." Jai added. "Back then I was a student out for a good time. Not now. We both really wanted you, we still do."

"But you still talk about this Izzy woman, and you were arguing."

Garth looked at her with a pleading expression. "We haven't talked about Izzy since we knew her, over ten years ago. You reminded us of that situation, yes, because she wanted a threesome with us. The difference is it didn't happen with Izzy, and it did happen with you."

When Faye took that on board, and remembered how he'd broken through his own personal barriers, she felt floored.

Garth sighed loudly and reached out for her hand. When she folded her arms across her chest, resisting him, he beckoned. "Please Faye. I need to touch you. This is driving me crazy."

Faye stared at his hand. If she took it, it would be fatal. She couldn't resist the big guy, and if he apologised and she let herself feel more than she already felt for them it would be harder still. This conversation had to happen, but when it was done she'd still have to walk away because she didn't want to come between them as friends and business partners.

Try as she might, she couldn't resist slipping her fingers into his large palm, and when he closed his hand over hers, it seemed to unravel some of the tension she carried. *He makes me feel safe*.

In that moment she saw it, clear as day. Jai was the one who set her loose and Garth was the one who kept her safe while she took the ride of her life.

Garth's grip grew tighter. Then he sat down and reeled her in.

Within a heartbeat Faye found herself sitting on his lap, tucked in against him. He held her close, not allowing her to break free.

"I'm so sorry we put you through this. We had no right to assume anything, we both said things we regret in the heat of the moment. It's not up to us who gets to keep seeing you. We can only hope that you will keep seeing us, at least one of us, or both of us. It's up to you." He drew back and looked into her eyes.

Jai sat down next to them. Their proximity made her melt.

She shook her head, stubbornly sticking to her plan. "I can't keep seeing you, either of you. It would jeopardise your friendship and your business partnership. I'm not going to do that. When I thought about it, once we'd got involved, I realised how much you both had at stake. All I risked was getting too involved and getting hurt."

"And having too good a time," Jai interjected.

"Shut up you, you always make things more difficult." Even as she said it she knew it wasn't true. Jai made things easier, and the humour in his comment made her smile and broke the tension. She sighed. "You're right, I was having a good time, but I would never forgive myself if I altered your friendship."

"Our friendship has been altered by you," Garth said, "but not in a bad way. Being around you made us realise what we're like. You were right, we are just like an old married couple, but it works for us. Having you there…it's crazy I know, but it felt like the three of us fitted together really well, and we both missed you like crazy when you were gone."

Faye took in the sincerity in their expressions.

"The other day, I lost it. I was afraid that you might want to see one of us, and it wouldn't be me. After only three days, the thought of that happening was doing my head in. I was prepared to fight for you. I'm so sorry that you heard us fighting. What was said was wrong and it was heat of the moment stuff."

"All we're asking," Jai said, "is that we wind the clock back. We have fun, we get to know each other some more, and we move forward together. If you'll have us?"

"Oh." Faye's eyes smarted. Maud's comments whispered around her mind. *Don't live with regrets. Hear them out.* Maud had been convinced Faye should stay with them. That's what she was saying, and she'd been privy to their private conversations.

"If we promise, Scouts' honour, not to fall out as friends, will you give it a go?"

"Say you will," Jai blurted.

"Okay, I'll think about it."

"Thank god!" Garth showered her face in kisses. "I really meant it when I said it was doing my head in."

Faye laughed, she couldn't help herself.

"What?"

"You do have a bit of a wild-eyed look about you."

"Yeah," Jai said, "like a mad dog, a hound that's been locked out and can't get to his beloved mistress."

"You didn't fare much better," Garth shot back. "He's been pacing around here like a scabby stray. He didn't use a comb for three days and the beard went wild."

Faye laughed. "Okay, okay, I get the message, if I don't check up on you from time to time you're going to scare away your clients, right?"

"That's it exactly." Jai winked at her.

"In that case, I'd better give it another go."

Chapter Eighteen

Cosseted between the two of them on Garth's bed, Faye pressed her head back into the pillows and savoured their hands on her. She felt free and high, like she was on a magic carpet, and the doubts that had clung to her were getting loose and flying off in the breeze. If she let them all go, this could be everything she'd ever dreamed of.

"I was thinking," Jai said, "if we merged the two top floors of the house into one unit we could make a home big enough for three, right above the business."

"So now you want to move in, now Faye is in the picture."

"Like I always say to you, the stars have to be in alignment."

"I thought we were taking it easy, winding the clock back, and you—the laid back one—are now making housey-housey plans."

Jai grinned. "Did I peak too soon?"

"It's fun to think about, but maybe you should get the business up and running before you redesign the building again." Faye couldn't help laughing.

"I notice the lady didn't say no," Jai said to Garth.

"You're happy, aren't you?" Garth nuzzled her neck.

"Mmnn. I just wish that I could have you both, at once, properly."

"You can," Jai responded with a more serious, focused tone, "it depends how you feel about anal sex."

Faye experienced a flood of arousal at his suggestion. Somewhat embarrassed, she lifted one shoulder. "I've never…I don't know."

Jai looked at Garth.

"It's not something I'm familiar with," Garth said.

Faye noticed that he looked a bit coy as well and was fixed on Jai as if for guidance.

"Not familiar with giving, or receiving?" Jai directed the question to Garth and grinned.

Garth narrowed his eyes. "One of these days you really will go too far."

Faye laughed softly. "My guess is that if he hasn't already gone too far in the last ten years, it's not going to happen." *Not now we're together.* She knew it deep in her heart, even though she didn't say it out loud.

Jai nodded. "Listen to our psychic girlfriend."

Our psychic girlfriend. Faye liked how that sounded. Apparently so did Garth because the tension in his expression vanished and he smiled at her.

Jai gave his approval. "That's better. Stop taking everything so seriously, Buddy. I wonder about you, really I do."

Garth rolled his eyes.

Having broken the tension, Jai wrapped his arm around Faye. It was a tender cuddle, and he kissed her softly on the mouth. "If you really want to try, and you're willing, then I'll take care of you."

Faye wilted against him. Every iota of energy in her body condensed into a hot spot in her groin. His loving, caring approach stole any last doubts away. She nodded her head.

Jai got up and went for his jacket.

When he returned he had a handful of condoms and a sachet of lube. And an erection.

"You look well prepared," Faye said.

Garth turned sideways and jammed his cock against her side, as if to let her know he was well prepared too.

Delighted, she squirmed against him. He locked one hand over her hip, holding her against his erection.

Faye watched as Jai tossed Garth a condom packet. Then he stood by the bed, rolled on a condom, then coated it in lube and put the sachet down on the bed. He encouraged her to face Garth, who was ready for her, sheathed cock and all.

He stroked her thighs. She opened them in response.

"Touch me," she begged.

His fingers slid against the wetness of her sex folds. She stroked his head. He nuzzled against her.

"Go on," Jai murmured, his body extending itself against hers, his mouth against her neck. "Don't stop there, give her all you've got." He chuckled softly. He pressed his erection against the seam of her bottom. It felt very slippery.

Faye gasped, completely aware of the male forces surrounding her. She closed her eyes and let the feeling of Garth's fingers questing through her wetness take her to heaven again. The hard, contained force at her bottom made her want penetration, double penetration.

Garth shifted his fingers inside her.

She began to move on them, her head falling back. "I want you both."

Garth moved so that he was between her legs, tucking her lower leg in line with his waist so as not to lie on it more heavily. Then his cock quickly found the wet niche between her legs.

Faye cried out with joy as he thrust inside her.

He drew back and lunged again.

She held him with her eyes, urging him on, swept up into his rhythm, molten inside, sensitised to every movement. "I want more," she cried out.

Garth swore under his breath.

"Shallow strokes a while," Jai instructed.

Garth nodded his way and slowed his pace. "You look so bloody good," Garth whispered.

Her core pounded, waves of pleasure surging through her.

Jai moved his cock to her anus, offering it to her. Faye nodded her head. She wanted to feel it fill her, she wanted his passion there.

"Do you still want more?" Jai asked her, his voice controlled.

Faye groaned, her body ricocheting with a riot of opposing signals. She was unable to form words.

"Yes?" he murmured, and she nodded her head, her hair trailing over her face as she did so, intoxicated with it, overwhelmed with shame, shame that flooded her sex when she was forced to concede that she did want more.

"Yes, I want you to fill me up," she blurted it out.

"Sweet Jesus," Garth said.

When he shifted down and angled his cock to her back passage it felt huge. Her body instinctively clamped, but Jai lubed his fingers and inserted one.

"Oh my god!"

He stroked his finger in and out, making her relax.

It felt so strange, but ludicrously good.

Then he replaced his finger with his cock, applying pressure. She wondered if she could ever manage it, but at the same time she wanted to impale herself on it.

"Ease down when you're ready," Jai whispered against her ear.

She pressed back, wanting to feel like she had with his finger in there while Garth filled her sex.

"Oh yes, that's it, nice and slow."

She stifled a moan, the girth of his cock seemed like too much, then he rode up a way inside her.

"Fuck!" She panted for breath. "So full!" A moment later she found her rhythm, taking in a good length of him—and an intake of breath—on each of his moves.

"That's it," Jai whispered, panting. "Oh yes, you're so good at this."

She could tell he held back, letting her find her way with it, and she also sensed how hard that was for him.

Garth obviously felt it too because he groaned and looked as if he could barely hold back. "Jesus, Jai, I can feel you too."

"It's nice that I can surprise you after all these years," Jai muttered.

She felt Garth's hands on her again, urgent, and he began to thrust deeper again as if the incredible fullness and the push and shove down there had taken him over as much as it had her. She wanted this so badly, she wanted to be filled and used by both of them, to be taken in every way.

Two lovers, she was having her two lovers both at once, better than all her fantasies put together. Already she was blossoming into orgasm. Her pelvis was awash with heat, her body shuddering.

Jai rubbed his hand over her breasts, his fingers hard against her peaked nipples. Faye felt feverish, weak and agitated all at the same time. She was so thoroughly pinioned. Her body went limp, able only to ride each wave of sensation. She began to come, very quickly, her body lifted up by her two lovers, her sex clenching and spasming.

Garth grunted, his body gleaming with sweat and taut with effort, his hips rolling. Jai panted at her back, his cock rock hard, at its most swollen as it finally shot its load.

Garth cursed loudly, then his cock began to jerk—once, twice, three times. He leaned over her, panting, and when she caught her breath again, she pulled him close, dizzy with pleasure.

"Satisfied, Madame?" Jai asked.

"Supremely."

Epilogue

It had been a long time since all three Evans sisters were able to gather together for coffee and toasted panini at Luigi's coffee house. Holly and Faye had kept up the tradition of meeting there once a fortnight while Monica was touring with her job, but it was good to be back again, all three of them at their favourite table by the window overlooking the busy pavements outside.

Faye savoured the moment. The reunion with her sisters after such an eventful year for them all meant a lot to her, and she stored away every precious moment for her memory bank. It was a gorgeous day, which made it even better. Although still cold, the sky was clear and the sun shone. The busy London street seemed to be filled with energy, the fast moving crowd of passers-by outside the window made vital by the breath of spring in the air. Inside, the smell of fresh coffee and good food surrounded them, as did the sound of happy chatter and laughter.

Faye took the opportunity to broach a question she'd been wondering about. "Do you think we've all been drawn to having two men in our lives because there are three of us, because we're used to having the support of two others and giving it to others?"

Holly sat back in her chair, her expression startled. "You might have something there. I'd not thought of that. What do you think, Monica?"

Monica nodded. "That's a very clever deduction, Sherlock."

Faye grinned. "So we've got an excuse for ignoring the norms now?"

"Do we need an excuse?" Monica looked quietly confident, as well she might, having had the longest to get used to being in a threesome.

"Well, no," Faye replied, "not as long as everyone is happy with the situation."

Holly tapped Faye on the forearm with one finger. "And are you and Garth and Jai happy with your situation now?"

"We're taking it one day at a time, but yes, we're happy." Even as she said it, her chest swelled with the emotion that triggered whenever she thought about her guys. They were working so hard for the relationship, as was she, and when it was good it was great. They still had teething troubles, but she was getting them to communicate without arguing, which seemed like a necessary shift, no matter how much they insisted it worked for them to be hounding each other.

"That's all anyone can do," Holly said, "and if you're all aiming for the same goal, it's got to be good. And the ghost, Maud?"

"Maud has gone. The one question that kept her lingering here was answered, and she was finally able to break free of her corporeal life." Faye smiled to herself. "I'll miss her."

"I hope I don't have a lingering question, when I kick the bucket," Monica reflected.

"What are you worried about?" Holly asked. "If you do linger Faye will be here to sort you out."

Faye laughed. "That's exactly what Jai said when Garth brought up the same issue."

Monica smiled. "You're forbidden to kick the bucket before any of us."

"I feel so needed and useful." Faye grinned. "I'll do my best to outlive you all." Stirring her coffee, she turned the conversation back on Monica. "So, tell us about the wedding plans, that's what we're here for."

"Well, Cumbernauld's will host the reception and everyone there wants to be involved, so that's pretty much out of my hands and taken care of. I need to think about our dresses next." She glanced at her younger sisters expectantly, a half smile hovering.

"No meringue frocks, please," Faye begged.

"You know me better than that." Monica looked as if she was enjoying their hesitation. "I meant to tell you, Aunt Josie actually said I should wear our grandmother's ivory silk wedding gown, can you believe it?" Monica shook her head.

Holly lifted her hands from her coffee cup and gestured broadly. "Cripes. They never get it, do they? Can you imagine the day you'd have, managing the memories that could come off that old family heirloom?"

"I know." Monica laughed. "According to Aunt Josie her cousin wore it and ran off with her ex in it."

Holly shook her head. "It doesn't bear thinking about."

"So what *are* you going to wear?" Faye looked at her older sister, wishing for a share of her calm approach to life, her utterly collected manner. It was partly a façade, she knew that. But it went deeper since Owen and Alec had come into her life. There used to be tension in Monica's posture, and she had always been buttoned-up—both on the outside and the inside.

That had changed. She still kept her hands loosely clasped together, but she was so much more relaxed. Her lovers had allowed her to become more comfortable with her exceptional psychic gift, simply because they understood how it functioned and worked around it. That had enabled her to travel the world safely in their care, and to take her career in new and exciting directions. Faye was so grateful. Of the three of them, Monica needed it the most.

"I'll pick up something simple and elegant," Faye reassured them, "with your help, I hope."

"And who is the best man going to be," Holly queried, "as if we needed to ask?"

"Yes, Alec will be best man." Monica gazed off into the distance, smiling to herself.

"Is he happy?" Faye was curious about each and every angle of her more experienced sisters' relationships, even though she knew hers would be different.

"He is. He says he couldn't be happier." Her eyelids lowered. She wiped the corner of her left eye quickly and laughed. "It's strange but I know it's true, he really means it."

"Makes me wish we'd done it that way," Holly said, "but there wasn't a natural or obvious way to do what we wanted, so we made our own ceremony."

Faye stared down into her coffee. When she'd told them about Monica's wedding, Jai had joked that she'd have to marry Garth if there was going to be a wedding for them, because Garth was the insecure one. It had seemed like a bit of fun at the time. It made sense though. Jai never really made throwaway remarks. It often appeared that he did, but the truth was he was a very good judge of human nature and he had a way of tuning in to people and bringing out their deepest desires. Even though Jai was a free spirit he'd led Garth to great things with his own business, whereas he might not have taken the risk alone. He'd triggered the ménage à trois affair between the three of them, subtly sensing what each of them needed from it. Even now, when they were all so much more chilled with each other, he knew when to put Garth in charge, and when to spur him on, provoking him to show his best side.

Faye still worried that it was somehow wrong—that it wouldn't last, and that she was in it because of her sisters and their joy—but when she stopped worrying about it and just enjoyed, their relationship was everything she could have wished for and more.

"Are you going to share those private thoughts of yours?" Holly asked.

Faye realised she'd been miles away. "Sorry. I was just thinking that if we end up half as happy as you guys, we'd be very happy indeed."

"I think you had a very good point," Holly responded, "about a three way relationship working for us. You've been our anchor in our troubled times, and you can be their anchor too."

"I hope so." She was about to say more about her hopes and doubts, but Gianni, their waiter, sidled in with their plates arranged along one arm.

"Three tempting dishes, for three tempting ladies," he stated as he placed the plates down. "Holly, Monica, and Faye."

"Is it any wonder we keep coming here," Holly said. "Your memory is amazing."

"With you three ladies it is so hard to forget," he murmured, oozing charisma. "Sisters too, wonderful." He took his fingers to his mouth and kissed them.

"Gianni, you're outrageous." Monica gave him one of her looks. It was supposed to be chastising, but Faye could see that it came across much more suggestively than it might have done a year ago.

Gianni bowed. "What I would really like to know is… are any of you ladies single?" He rested his hand on the back of Faye's chair.

She turned in her seat to look up at him, intrigued.

"I have two brothers," he added, "if all of you are free."

Both Faye and Holly looked to their older sister, the one who could keep a straight face.

"Two brothers as well?" Monica took a deep breath and looked for all the world as if she was genuinely contemplating the idea. "Well, that's very tempting, but I'm afraid none of us are in a position to be tempted." She exchanged glances with Holly and Faye. "I'm sorry, Gianni, none of us are single."

Faye knew what she was thinking. *None of us is even double. We are more than a couple, we're something else—something stronger, something individual and unique to every one of us. A committed ménage a trois.*

Faye took strength from her older sisters. They gave her faith and hope. Her own relationship may or may not work in the long-term, but each and every one of them was doing their best to make it work.

That was what life was all about, working for what meant the most, and Faye lifted her cup, sipped her coffee and anticipated everything else it had to bring.

*

If you enjoyed this novel please consider leaving a rating or review.

ABOUT THE AUTHOR

Saskia Walker is an award-winning British author of erotic fiction. Her short stories and novellas have appeared in over one hundred international anthologies including Best Women's Erotica, The Mammoth Book of Best New Erotica, Secrets, and Wicked Words. Her erotica has also been featured in several international magazines including Cosmo, Penthouse, Bust, and Scarlet. Fascinated with seduction, Saskia loves to explore how and why we get from saying "hello" to sharing our most intimate selves in moments of extreme passion. After writing shorts for several years Saskia moved into novel-length projects. Her erotic single titles include The Burlington Manor Affair, Rampant, Reckless and the Taskill Witches trilogy: The Harlot, The Libertine and The Jezebel. Her novels Double Dare and Rampant both won Passionate Plume awards and her writing has twice been nominated for a RT Book Reviews Reviewers' Choice Award. Nowadays Saskia is happily settled in Yorkshire, in the north of England, with her real-life hero, Mark, and a houseful of stray felines. You can visit her website for more info. www.saskiawalker.co.uk

If you enjoyed this novel you might enjoy INESCAPABLE.

When Lily Howard agrees to meet the man she is having a powerfully erotic online affair with, she subsequently walks into a crime scene. Sexy police officer Seth Jones takes her into witness protection together with her online lover, Adrian Walsh, a man with crucial evidence for a court case.

Deep in the heart of the Welsh countryside and locked up in a secluded hideaway with these two men — one alpha dominant policeman, and a wry, sensitive accountant who knows her every secret erotic desire — Lily soon becomes embroiled in a torrid ménage a trois that surpasses her every fantasy. Lily is wildly empowered by living her innermost desires in the safety of the hideaway. Adrian is the key that unlocks her sexuality, and Seth is the master who sets them both free.

As danger stalks ever closer and the three lovers are torn apart, they each find that deep emotional bonds have also been forged. Can Lily ever forget what they shared? Does she even want to?

FAYE'S SPIRIT

"With a scene-stealing opening, three strong main leads, some interesting secondary characters, a few unexpected twists in this intriguing plot, and some very passionate scenes, Inescapable makes for a very satisfying read. Get your copy now!" 5 stars from Just Erotic Romance Reviews

Available now in print and digital format.

Visit www.saskiawalker.co.uk for more details on Saskia's other works. Thank you for reading!

Printed in Great Britain
by Amazon